BEAUTIFUL *Mistake*

BEAUTIFUL *Mistake*

JYOTI DHANOTA

1st Edition
2023

Beautiful Mistake is a work of fiction. Names, characters, places, and incidents are either the product of the author's imagination or are used fictitiously. Any resemblance to actual persons, living or dead, events, or locales is entirely coincidental.

First paperback edition January 2023

BOOK COVER DESIGN | Christine Cover Designs
BOOK LAYOUT | GR Book Covers
AUTHOR PHOTO | Brenda Mia Photography

♡

To everyone that grew up wishing for love.

Author's note

This book is the sequel to *Beautiful Consequence.* It is recommended that you read that novel before this one. This book also contains characters from *The Chaos Within Us* and *The Chance We Took.* If you don't want spoilers, it is suggested those books are read first.

Varun

Chapter I

The atmosphere was as intense as the staring contest we were basically holding. The gloomy weather added to the intensity as we kept our eye contact. I wanted to know the answer to this question since the night Riya was in the hospital.

Seems like neither of us are going to back down, I thought. *Time to just go back into "best friend" mode instead of this "intense" mode.*

"Tell me what you did in college," I repeated.

Vihaan had been my best friend since kindergarten. I had been by his side for the majority of his life (give or take the couple of months that he hated my guts). I had deserved that, though, considering what I had done to his girlfriend.

"I'm telling you I didn't do anything," he said.

"It had to have been something. Did you cheat on an exam? Did you cheat on an assignment? Were you on academic probation? No, you are too smart for that. Did you cuss a professor out? Did you get a C in a class? Bro, that's okay because C's get degrees! Did you flunk your final? Did you miss an assignment? Were you late to class three times causing your grade to go down by one letter? Wait, I think that's if you missed class. What did you do?"

"No, no, no, hell no, too smart for that, also too smart for that, nope, and lastly, no."

We were currently at his place for the weekend. He switched his schedule around to have more time with Anaya, but he ended up having more time with me. I loved that I got to rub it in his face because Anaya worked as a store manager full-time, and with her rotating schedule, she was usually working when he wasn't. There had been a few times where they had time together, though. If her freelance job would have worked out, they probably could have been together more often.

"Oh, come on!" I whined. "I thought we don't keep secrets from each other anymore."

"You need an off button." He had been saying that he would find my off button since our school days, but I had always just been very stubborn. "Riya should have ran away when she had the chance. You don't pester her this way."

"I wouldn't even dare to do that."

"I will tell you," he finally gave in. "I had another best friend in college from my public speaking class. We just vibed really well, but I didn't tell you because you would have come crying to me like you did when you thought Amber was going to replace you."

Hilarious. I thought we agreed to never bring Amber or Camren back up during our time left on this planet.

"You cheated on me?" I gasped. "How dare you have another best friend. You can have other friends, but I am your only best friend. Got it?"

I'm not talking to him. He is on best-friend-timeout until he realizes that he can't replace me, ever.

Vihaan burst out laughing, "I knew you would react like that. It's the only reason I made that lie up, but at least

I got you to stop talking. I'll make a note to myself that replacing you will be your off button."

"Don't even think about it. We already had months without each other, and I won't let you do it again. I will tell Anaya you were threatening to end our friendship."

Vihaan and Anaya were such a beautiful couple. After everything they had gone through, they were still standing strong next to each other. They weren't even looking for a serious relationship when they had started dating, but now if you utter a word against her, Vihaan wouldn't even think, he would kill you no questions asked. Anaya was a very caring and down-to-earth person herself. The main thing about her that stuck with me was her forgive-don't-forget mindset.

Over half of his menu in these past three years had changed to her favorites so she didn't have to think about what she wanted to eat while visiting him.

"She will reply with the fact that you actually worked on ending it," Vihaan smirked.

I sighed, "Can't win here. I am going home, where I also can't win any arguments, so bye. You will see when you get married that your wife is always right. Even when she's wrong, she is right."

"That's because you have to do everything she says. You did that to yourself because if you didn't fuck shit up that day, you could be getting away with shit now, not that I am encouraging you to ever get away with anything. I do tell Riya everything myself if I suspect you are about to misbehave."

I hate him. I am going to go replace him instead and look for another best friend. I am sure I will find one just walking around in a grocery store somewhere. We deadass said we won't bring that up again. Riya still does when we get into an argument, and that is how she wins every fucking time. Every! Fucking! Time!

I dramatically grabbed my things. "I am going home, sir!"

Vihaan hated it when I called him "sir" since we were only three weeks apart in age. He deserved that right now, though.

"Bye," he said, trying not to laugh.

I sighed at his behavior before heading home. I knew he was messing around, so I didn't hold it against him.

My parents were home, along with my brother, Ash, who was on winter break from college. Riya was probably stuck in commuter traffic at the moment then. She had told me that she hated her job, which I found hilarious because she wanted to work more than anything prior to us getting married. Now, everyday I get to hear, "I hate my job," as soon as she walks in or when the two of us are alone. She can quit. I told her a million times, but she is stuck on the fact that she is earning her own money.

Friday nights are pizza and game nights with the family, since we couldn't go out for a walk during the harsh, cold east winters. It became a tradition since the first winter Riya suggested it after we got married. Three years later, we still did this every Friday in the winter, unless we had an event to attend or it was a holiday. We played for money, which got everyone to be more competitive with each other, but nobody ever cheated during the games. Our family placed an important value on honesty.

When we all felt we had played enough, everyone would go into their rooms. I knew my parents would sleep, my brother would work on studying anything he could to prepare for his board exams, since he wanted to be a psychologist. He would be finishing his BA this year, but he was always studying. The next step for him was to get a doctoral degree. He said he wanted to start studying now so he wouldn't have to cram everything. Riya and I would either spend the time talking about our day or watching a movie before going to bed. The weather for today called for a movie, and since Christmas was next week, we had chosen to watch a holiday film before calling it a night.

Varun

Chapter 2

Christmas morning was welcomed with snow and love. As a family, we celebrated Christmas wearing our matching pajama sets, which differed yearly. This year, they were white with gingerbread men on both the top and bottom, with a brown border around the bottom of the arms. I was sure this tradition would continue until we ran out of ideas for what to wear.

Our breakfast was pancakes with some sort of Christmas representation. Last year, Riya made pancakes that looked like Rudolph. Today, they looked like Santa. She had strawberries on the top for the hat, some whip cream for the bottom of the hat, chocolate chips for the eyes, and bananas for the beard.

Riya had always done so much for Christmas. She always had the house (both internally and externally) decorated, made breakfast on Christmas morning, dinner on Christmas Eve, and started collecting toys for toy drives as early as October. All I was responsible for was the Christmas tree, which was the only decoration in this house prior to our marriage.

I understood she did it because she never got to experience it growing up. She had told me that she was usually locked in her room while everyone else got to enjoy the holiday. She never had a Christmas gift until our first one together. Thirty years in the making, I could never stop her from healing her inner child. It's why I spoiled her on our first Christmas with at least fifty presents. I could have done more, but the others would not have had anything to give her. I told her to make a list of what she wanted and got her everything on that list. I should have waited because now, after two years, I had no idea what to get. Her list mainly stayed the same. I decided to do a little DIY project as a gift for her. On her birthday after our roka, Mom said she liked the walk-in closet, so I told her that would be her present. I would have given it away if I had started working on it prior.

We would have lunch with Vihaan and Anaya today, which had also become a tradition. Before our partners were in our life, Vihaan and I usually had a sleepover on Christmas Eve. From the time we met in kindergarten to now, Vihaan and I had not had a Christmas apart.

After we opened our presents, we usually decorated some cookies or made a gingerbread house. However, this year, one of my cousins had a kid after years of trying, so my parents would be going there to celebrate the baby's first Christmas. My brother was meeting up with some of his friends, and we were going to Vihaan's place. Instead, we all worked on a two-thousand-piece jigsaw puzzle, which took us almost until my parents (who Riya now referred to as "our" parents) had to leave just to finish.

"Princess, what the hell is this?" I asked when I saw a suitcase on the bed.

I don't like the smirk on her face. She has something up her sleeve right now.

"Remember when you bought me fifty things?" she asked, grinning ear to ear.

"Riya. No. We talked about this. You don't have to make up for that. I don't need a suitcase full of gifts. The only thing I need is for you to always be happy and healthy."

"Is it because I am a lot to deal with when I get sick?" she asked.

I won't let her ever think about what her parents told her growing up.

"No, you are not a lot to deal with. Forget anyone ever told you that. I don't like it because you ask me to stay away from you or I'll get sick. Then, you go to sleep in the guest room, and I don't get my cuddles." I pouted.

She laughed as she told me just to open it. I did. It wasn't a suitcase full of gifts but a record player.

Vintage! I love it! I just have to hunt down some pieces of vinyl now.

"I love it. Thank you, princess," I said, kissing her.

"There's also something else, but I can't give you that yet. There is a better time for it. Give me about a week."

"How is that fair? I only got one thing, which will take me time to finish."

"It's fair, husband. You got fifty things at once! Now, you aren't just going to make a walk-in closet. I know you will have that filled with dresses, jewelry, heels, sneakers, office wear, and traditional wear."

That was supposed to be a surprise.

She added, "Just like how you didn't only buy me the vanity but filled it up with makeup and perfumes."

I see how she got to that conclusion now. She deserves to be spoiled.

Everything she didn't have for thirty years, she was going to get now.

"Anyways, we should get going. Who knows how much traffic we are going to run into. Should we go just like this? In our matching PJs?" She fidgeted with excitement.

"It's snowing outside!"

She was going to get sick, and then, we couldn't share a bed. No, thank you.

"So? The car has a heater. They'll have the heat on at home too."

"Riya-"

I got cut off by the only statement that always helps her win and makes anything go her way: "Remember what you did with Camren? You owe me."

"Fine. We can freeze to death in our PJs."

She would always have the upper hand after my confession. This was her revenge. I had a feeling she'd get revenge. I didn't know that it would be lifelong and she'd win every argument because of it.

I didn't miss how she shook as we stepped outside the car. I wanted to call her out but decided it was in my favor not to say a word. I cranked both the music and heater up as we drove off.

Vihaan didn't live too far from me. He was about an hour away after he and Anaya had moved to their current single-story home.

"Hi Esha," I said, almost surprised that she opened the door. This is the same person who never left her room or spoke to anyone due to trauma.

"Don't act all surprised— Anaya encouraged me to go to therapy. I can't thank my brother enough for having a girlfriend like her. If you don't want to be paralyzed by the cold, I suggest you come inside," she said.

Riya almost ran inside, but I couldn't get over the fact that Esha was finally healing! This was the longest conversation I had had with her.

Props to her for taking steps to heal.

"Look who decided to show up." Vihaan grinned as I walked inside.

"Sir, your sister can talk now!"

Vihaan laughed. "She could always talk, dumbass. She just talks more now, fortunately. Unfortunately, she is very sassy and uses her words to bully me even more than she did before. It's nice to see her talk to people that aren't just Mom or me. All these years, I tried to do anything I could to help her. Anaya told her once to try therapy, and now look at Esha."

Speaking of Anaya, where was she? She should have been here by now.

Riya seemed to have the same thought because she asked where Anaya was.

"They're in Esha's room. I haven't been to Esha's room as much as she has and I grew up with her! That's unfair. I am replaced by my girlfriend," Vihaan whined.

I took the chance to mess with them. "I know how you feel. Riya replaced me with my brother."

"But you deserve to be replaced at any given second. Isn't that right, Riya?" My best friend asked my wife.

I should have thought about who I would mess with before I did.

"Exactly!" Riya said as they high-fived each other.

Anaya joined right that second and I whined that I hated her boyfriend.

She chuckled, "You and I both."

"Oh! What did he do? I can kick his ass for you!" I said, intrigued.

"I forgot that she's allergic to honey and I may have added it to one of the dishes. I may have asked her to try. It was a complete accident," Vihaan answered instead.

"You almost killed her!" Riya and I exclaimed.

"Hey! You, out of all people, can't say that to me," Vihaan said, looking at me.

I was wrong. Both Riya and Vihaan will spend a lifetime using everything against me. Not just Riya.

"It's fine. I'm fine. It wasn't a major reaction," Anaya said, easing the tension.

Since Vihaan was working on making something, now would be the best time to give my Michelin Star best friend his present. Riya had no idea what I got him, so when he opened it, the four of us began laughing since Esha had now joined.

I thought he would be annoyed, but instead, he played into it. "Oh my God! A cookbook! For me? You shouldn't have."

"Damn it! I wanted you to be like, 'Really, a cookbook?' Not the response I was hoping for."

The girls were still laughing as Vihaan set the table after putting the book down.

He had made sliders, baked baby potatoes, cranberry meatballs, stuffed mushrooms, mini quiches, and curried crab spread. We were the ones that told him not to make a lot of stuff, but he still did.

The five of us ate together as his mom visited a relative. She quickly said hi to us before she ran out. This may be a yearly tradition, but considering all the embarrassing stories Vihaan told Riya about me during childhood, I might end it this year. Maybe not because I do love to see my favorite people. I hope he knows I can and will pull the same shit. Just watch when he comes over for New Year.

CHAPTER 3

I WOKE UP ON MY DAY OFF TO A BED THAT WASN'T EMPTY. Finally, we both got a day to sleep and wake up next to each other.

I still had nightmares about my past. All the abuse I had gone through kept me up at night. I kept that to myself. Varun had found me covered in puddles of my own blood that night, beaten and tortured my parents and brothers.

My family had found out we had eloped. They had threatened to harm me, but what could they do when deported? They couldn't harm me when we lived in different countries. I felt safe knowing that.

I no longer had to worry about pulling myself out of dark places. I had the support of not just my husband but my in-laws, Anaya and Vihaan. They all knew my story. Anaya was my best friend now. I never had the chance to have one of those growing up, and she made sure we lived up to all the years I'd missed because of it. It worked out since Vihaan and Varun were best friends.

"Good morning, princess. I see you didn't go to work today. Smart move," Varun said, kissing me on the forehead.

"I'm off today."

"So am I. What are we doing? Should we spend the day out, or would you prefer a day in? I can make dinner reservations. We can go to a movie."

"I have a girls' day with Anaya," I lied.

He pouted. "Unfair. You get one day off, and you choose Anaya over me?"

I nodded in an effort to keep going.

He turned to grab his phone. I became curious to see what he was doing, so I moved closer. I couldn't help but want to laugh when I saw him pull up Vihaan's number.

"Bestie!" Varun greeted.

I just knew Vihaan was sighing on the other end. These two had a friendship where one of them had a sunshine, golden retriever energy and the other one, Vihaan, got stuck with the ball of energy.

"Isn't today a beautiful day to take your girlfriend on a date? Surprise her with a plan! Take her out," my husband continued.

Really? Have you seen the way Vihaan looks at Anaya? He doesn't need to be told when to take her on a date. He probably takes her on one every other day. He's crazy about her. He refers to her as the most beautiful consequence of his life whenever she's not around. It really is when I see them together. Definitely made for the other, I thought.

"So? You can't take her on another one?"

Silence as Vihaan spoke.

"I know the girls have a day out together! That's why I'm asking. Come on, after everything I did for you, you can't ask Anaya to cancel for me?"

That was probably not the best thing for Varun to say to Vihaan. But there was a pause. Why was Vihaan saying the girls had a day out? I was joking about that.

"Sir, I'll get on my knees and kiss your feet."

This was what best friends since kindergarten sounded like. I didn't know how Vihaan kept him around so long, but props to him. I should get that man some spa time or something.

"Love you, bestie. Muah!"

Varun hung up the call, and I had to question exactly why Vihaan took him back. He had the opportunity to never be with him again. It was his chance to leave him, so why didn't he stick to that decision forever?

Varun turned to me, "You're stuck with me."

"Has Vihaan ever told you that you're annoying?" I asked.

"All the time. I just don't care because he's Vihaan. It's his way of saying he loves me. Like now, when I said I love him, he replied, 'I wonder if God would thank me for returning his annoying creation.' We've been best friends since elementary school and are in our thirties now. He has to love me to stick around so long."

I was still laughing at 'returning the annoying creation.' I could just imagine Vihaan saying, "This one is broken. He talked nonstop and didn't come with an Off button."

"Princess, what do you want to do today?"

"I'm okay with a day indoors, but since the weather's nice, can we at least go bike riding?"

Almost everyone I mentioned that was in my corner now was also making sure I got to do the things I never did as a child. For example, I never had my own bike. My parents thought I didn't need one, but all three of my brothers did. I should have taken one of theirs and run away from home.

"Of course. We can reward ourselves by going to the ice cream shop that just opened up. I know we both love to support small businesses."

"Sounds like a plan." I smiled.

He left to take a shower since it was his turn to make breakfast while I pulled my journal out. I tried to list things I'd want to do throughout the day but failed miserably at keeping up. I had notes from my therapist as well. I found it beneficial to take notes as she spoke so I could visit them as needed. My favorite was the emotional cup, where we discussed what fills my cup and what drains it. Positive things—such as love, affection, music, attention—filled the cup while negative things, like failing and rejection, emptied it.

Varun had seen me working on it, and I told him everything I put in the journal. Within the next hour, he handed me a paper with the alphabet with each letter highlighted and items under that letter that could make me happy. He was the one to tell me that self-care was not selfish. To this day, I have yet to find the right word to explain how safe I felt with him. Happy, for sure, but safe. I never knew what either of those felt like until he came into my life.

I still hold what he told me on our Roka day against him. It was the easiest way to win an argument.

Varun left, saying he was going to make an omelet for breakfast. I was fine with that. We could use the protein.

Once I was done with my shower and my morning yoga, I joined everyone for breakfast. With the five of us—his parents, his brother, and us—everyone had a day they'd make breakfast so others could sleep in. Usually, everyone worked, so you'd just have to wake up a bit earlier than your usual time. On the weekends, whoever wanted to cook could. It tended to be the first person up, which was seldom me. It wasn't because I didn't want to. Varun would change the time in our room back an hour and a half, so I always thought I could sleep some more. He'd take my phone too. I figured it out when I almost missed my dentist appointment. I was trying to figure out how I didn't pick it up earlier.

"I have my eye appointment this week. It's been bothering me," I told him after breakfast while washing the dishes.

"I still can't believe you won't listen to me. I have a degree for eyeballs!"

I scoffed, "You won't be professional."

"Princess, I'm always professional."

"You know what I mean. You'll say things like 'you have the most beautiful eyes' and shit like that."

"You do have the most beautiful eyes. I don't flirt with my patients though. It would be different for you because you're my wife."

"See! That's why I'm going to a different eye doctor. Not the one I'm married to!"

"Can't believe you are just going to cheat on me like that," he said.

I turned the water off to look at him. He realized what he said as soon as I did that. He quickly defended, "I didn't mean it like that. I meant my profession. I wouldn't even charge you. I still think artificial tears might help your eyes feel better. I'll shut up now."

"Mm-hmm."

He should be on a sports team since he played defense so well. He got lucky Vihaan called him right then and there. However, this time I made him put the call on speaker.

I didn't say anything. This conversation was just between the two men.

"Vihaan! I love you!" Varun couldn't hide how thankful he was.

"You have got to stop saying that to me. I'm not saying it back."

"You love me. I know you do."

"Anyways, I called because your dumb ass didn't tell me when we'd meet to drop my brother off tomorrow."

"Ah, right! His flight is at 10:25 p.m., so we can meet up around seven, go for dinner, and then go from there."

"Perfect. Bye."

"How dare you want to hang up so fast. I'm offended."

"Seriously, how does Riya put up with you?" Vihaan asked.

I answered, "Lots of yoga and wine."

"You two can't gang up on me. I'm hanging up."

Varun frowned before Vihaan actually disconnected it.

I was laughing so much I had to hold my stomach. Yep, I'm definitely in a much happier and safer place now. I wish the past me knew how happy the future me would be.

Varun

Chapter 4

If my friends answered my questions, that would be lovely. I was supposed to head out to Sweden tomorrow. I was going to attend some conference which I honestly could do without, but hey, a free trip for the optometrist in the area, sign me up.

I didn't recheck my phone until lunchtime since today was back-to-back, nonstop. I usually only worked on an appointment-only basis until it hit me that people were really busy, so I started accepting walk-ins. This way, they could go with what worked best for them.

Procrastination Station 🚆

Riya: Sorry I didn't reply earlier. Work

Anaya: I was cooking.

Vihaan: Can my reason for ignoring him be that I just wanted to ignore him?

Varun: Vihaan you on thin ice buddy -_-

Vihaan: Ask me if I care.

Riya: Anyways to answer your question around 5°. I did my research but idk if it's Celsius or not.

Vihaan: Can't believe you're going to the Ice Hotel. Such a big boy. They grow up so fast he started to do things all alone

Varun: 

I locked my phone and began going through any paperwork that I needed to finish. I had told Riya that I'd be home late because I was the type of person that didn't want to have anything left behind when he went somewhere. I wasn't closing the place. Another doctor would be taking walk-ins only. I made sure my assistant, Angie, didn't schedule any appointments for the week I'd be away.

Whoever was texting me had better be important. The times my phone buzzed under the mountain of papers were getting annoying.

Riya: Okay, the most important person in my life, so I'll have to look. My parents even know they've been replaced as the top priority.

Riya: They're being awkward

Riya: Something had to have happened

Riya: Anaya hates cooking

Riya: It's the main reason she said yes

Riya: Even Vihaan was off. I get it's a text but he didn't seem to joke the way he normally does with you

Riya: I called Anaya while you 2 were texting and she said it's nothing. I was probably reading into the text

Riya: I'm done bothering you. You probably have a mountain of paperwork. I love you. See you at home ♥

See, this was why I hated texting. Tone. We couldn't understand a person's tone through text the way we could while we spoke to them. I also felt something had been off with Vihaan. I thought it was about him getting news that his father had passed away, but it couldn't be. His dad was only abusive and then never in the picture. He hated him.

I opened my phone again and dialed the other number, instead deleting Vihaan's.

"Hello," Anaya answered.

"Do you have a minute?" I asked. I know I was the person who made Vihaan hate my guts at one point. I was the person who'd do anything to ensure he was not upset.

"I know absolutely nothing about Sweden."

"It's not about that. Is everything with you and Vihaan okay? You hate cooking, and he always does it for you. He loves to do that for you."

"I just felt like making something at home. The restaurant is a bit far from me. I despise driving in the snow. It scares the shit out of me."

Oh. That made so much more sense. I'd let Riya know before she started worrying about her and my best friend.

"Ah. I just wanted to know that. The text threw me off," I told her.

"It's okay. Vihaan's your best friend, so I'm not surprised you were worried. I was surprised you called me over him."

I lied and said, "Who said I didn't call him?"

"True. I have to call my family back in Oregon, so I'll hang up now. Bye."

She hung up almost immediately after using that excuse. I was confused, but for now, I could call Riya.

"Hi, princess," I greeted.

"I thought you'd be busy, so I didn't call."

"I saw your text and called Anaya. She said it's because the restaurant is far and she didn't want to drive in the snow."

"Oh! See, that makes much more sense. Those two love each other so much. I probably read too into the text. I feel better knowing that already. I love you. See you at home, and thank you for doing that."

"I love you too. I'll try to be home by dinner, but no promises."

"Sounds good," she said before disconnecting the call.

Most of my paperwork was referrals for surgery. I tried to share the workload with my assistants. Nobody liked a manager, super, or boss who didn't do the work. Nobody wanted to do the work while the person above just watched. That was a shitty person in charge.

My following appointment was with a child, a second-grader who loved to talk. I knew more about her than any other child in the first ten minutes.

Riya was right. We didn't need children. I was fine with spending my six-figure salary on my wife and me. Well, my family, too but Riya was my number one priority. Plus, who would want children in this economy?

"I need you to cover your right eye now and read me the letters," I told the child.

"That's easy. I know all my ABCs. We learned them in kindergarten. I'm in second grade," she said with pride.

How was I so tempted to not be professional and ask her to read just the bottom line?

"You know, when my mommy hits me, then it makes my eyes hurt from crying. I think that's why I have to come with broken glasses. Sometimes she hits really hard."

She said what now?

Her mom stiffened and pretended to laugh. "She's messing around. I don't hit her."

Yeah, uuumm, no . . . we're getting the cops right now. Not because I was the optometrist and it was required on that end, but every resident of New Jersey was a mandated reporter.

"Tell the doctor I don't hit you, honey."

How could I get the child to prove it? I had sent a quick text to Angie to call the cops on a child abuse case while the mom was trying to get the kid to say she didn't.

I was not going to stand here and not take action. She was a little kid! I was doing this because it was required. I mean, I still would do it regardless, but I saw Riya in her—little Riya who suffered abuse all her life until we found each other.

Riya had told me that when doctors suspected something, she had to say she fell or she'd be beaten worse. She had wanted to tell her school teacher or psychologist when it had gotten to the point she started to miss assignments. However, she had been afraid the torture would worsen, so she never said anything. She had told me I was the first to find out because she felt safe enough to tell me.

I couldn't let this little girl go her entire life getting hurt. I wasn't going to allow that. The Division of Child Protection and Permanency (DCPP) would start their investigation afterward, and they only had a specific time frame. Who knew what would happen to the child in that time frame? I wish I could take her home, but I know DCPP would need to talk with the child. The absolutely stunning thing was that New Jersey gave children rights as well. Basically, if she had to go to court, this child would have a lawyer through OLG to represent her.

I gave the cops, who finally decided to show up, the information I heard and what I witnessed. They told me they'd take it from there and took the mom and child outside. It was all on the cops and DCPP now.

I went back to my office after apologizing for the wait. Patients saw what was happening, so many of them didn't mind. I grabbed my phone to send Riya a quick text reminding her that I loved her before returning to work.

My day, thanks to that delay, didn't come to an end until 5:54 p.m. I finished all my paperwork, made a note to pay my employees two hours' worth of overtime, even if it was just one, and headed home.

When I walked in through the front door, I was greeted with another hug so tight I thought I'd stop breathing.

"You scared me! You texted out of the blue that you love me and never replied to my message!"

I was not even surprised. This was Riya's way of showing concern. She yelled at me whenever she was worried.

"Something happened at work. I'll tell you about it later," I said. "Plus, I can say I love you whenever I want. I won't be seeing you for seven days."

"You'll still be able to talk to me."

"I'm asking again if you want to come along."

"Nope. Maybe some other time," she said.

I nodded. I had a list of places we needed to visit since she never got to go anywhere as a child. Anaya had taken her to New York every December. It became a tradition for the girls to go on whatever weekend they were free, which meant Vihaan and I also started something. We weren't as fun as going to a different state, but we'd meet up and hit the casino. The only rule was that the girls couldn't find how much money we had lost. They never even asked.

I had taken a nice, warm shower before having dinner with my family. My parents kept asking if I packed correctly, who was dropping me off, and if I packed enough. It was cute they were worried, but I was an adult. I got this.

I was definitely going to miss home-cooked meals though. I hoped the food there tasted good. It was my first time going anywhere alone. I was both excited and nervous.

After dinner, I went to our room to ensure I had my bags ready. The flight would leave at 7:15 a.m. tomorrow, and I wanted to get as much sleep as possible. I didn't want to stress in the morning and forget something.

"Ready to go?" Riya asked as she walked in.

"I'm going to miss you the most."

"I know. What did you want to talk about earlier? What happened at work?"

I asked Riya to take a seat as I took her hand. This was a sensitive subject for her. I told her everything from how I thought the kid talked a lot all the way to the cops showing up.

"I can't say thank you enough. You have no idea how much I wished someone would have done that for me. You could have saved her life," she said, hugging me.

"I thought of you when it happened. That's why I sent the text."

"See, that makes more sense."

"I love you, Riya. You really did make me turn into a better person. Not that I was a villain before you. I mean, I had a villain phase. We don't talk about that."

Riya found the best way to get me to be quiet was by kissing. It worked every single time. Since I wasn't going to see her for a week, we should take advantage of each second we had today. Who needs sleep anyways?

Chapter 5

My palms were sweating, and I was positive my heartbeat was high enough to have me in the ER. I was nauseous with the amount of fear going on.

I was sitting downstairs when I got the text message. I made the decision right then and there to not tell Varun anything. I'd handle this on my own. I was a strong, independent woman.

"*Bhabi*, you want to go watch a movie?" I heard Ash ask from the kitchen.

We hung out often when Varun wasn't around. He usually did it so I wouldn't miss my husband all day.

"You look terrified. I'm telling my brother," he said when he came over and saw my current form.

"No!"

He went speechless at how quickly and loudly that came out.

"I mean, you don't have to tell him. It's nothing big. I'll let him know when he comes back."

He just left this morning. I didn't want him to come back right away. He'd make the pilot turn around if anything was happening to me. He definitely fell in love harder.

Ash seemed to dismiss it. "Okay. So movies?"

"Sure. Let me grab my purse," I told him and left to get it.

My phone went off with another text. With my hands trembling, I looked at it.

X: Did you think your husband was going to protect you

X: He's not even in the country

X: We have people watching you

X: Be very careful

I screenshotted all the text messages and phone number. I'd have to call my mobile carrier and report it to law enforcement later. An offense of malicious communication occurred as soon as the text was sent, so law enforcement should be able to do something about it. They'd be charged for sending it regardless of whether it'd been read. I could mark these messages as unread if I wanted to, but I'd let them think it was not affecting me.

I shook my thoughts off, put on a brave, happy face, and went back downstairs. I asked Ash if there was a comedy out and he said yes, so we'd watch that.

I was not going to let anyone know that I received a threat. I'd have it handled by this evening.

Chapter 6

It'd been three days since Varun had gone to Sweden—the most silent three days of my life since I married him. I missed his noisy moments so much. Only four more days until I could be with him again.

Varun was constantly sending me pictures of himself—not Sweden, himself. His excuse was that he didn't want me to be missing him. I told him I wanted photos of anything else, and he spammed me with selfies. I thought about blocking him for a few minutes but decided against it. He'd hop on the first flight back to ensure I unblocked him.

I didn't go to work today as I was having horrible period pain. I hated periods. I was sure every person with a uterus would agree. For me, I never got the feminine care I needed. Growing up, my mother had tossed out the pads I'd taken from school since she never bought me any. She told me it was my fault for being selfish and wanting to spend her money on pads. They'd been horrible for as long as I could remember. Even after marriage, I didn't dare to speak about the pain. That would change today.

I grabbed my phone and felt like the biggest bitch in the world as I called Anaya.

"Hi, Riya!" she cheerfully greeted me. "You didn't go to work?"

"Anaya, I'm so sorry to do this to you out of all people, but my period is unbearable. Varun isn't home, and my mother-in-law is at her cousin's. Any chance you take me to the hospital?"

"I'll be right over. You don't have to apologize for that by the way. What happened to me was just a jealous woman and a doctor that ended up losing his license."

We didn't talk about Amber or Camren anymore. None of the four of us brought them up.

"Thank you."

I found the strength to get out of bed and get dressed. I really could only wish it wasn't something serious. I really hoped Anaya wouldn't think badly of me for calling her. I knew she said it was okay on the phone, but what if it was something horrible?

My phone rang as soon as I was done. It was Varun calling.

"Hi," I said. "Missing me?"

"When am I not? How are you, princess?"

"Horrible. That time of the month," I told him.

"Oh. I wish I could be there for you, but, princess, I want you to get checked. It's not normal to have lots of pain."

I wanted to hide everything from him about the hospital but decided to let him know. I even mentioned whom I was taking.

"There's a surgical procedure called endometrial ablation. If you get diagnosed with fibroids, I want you to look into that. I remember some stuff I learned in school. It'll take maybe about two weeks to heal after surgery."

I had one question that had been bothering the shit out of me. In the three years we'd been married, we talked about wanting kids when the time came. What if I couldn't give him that? Would he leave me?

"What if I can't . . ." I couldn't bring myself to ask that question. I quickly covered my mouth so he wouldn't know I was crying.

"Then we adopt. I need you more than I need anyone or anything else. If they tell you the safest option is a hysterectomy, get it. I love you, Riya. Regardless of anything and everything. Now, please stop crying. I'm not stupid. I know you're crying."

I was so grateful he was understanding. I didn't even have to finish that sentence. I told him that I loved him and would wait for him before making a big decision. He only told me not to wait because it could get worse.

Anaya had shown up with my favorite food and drinks. I wasn't in the mood to have breakfast earlier, so this was really needed.

We arrived at the hospital about twenty minutes later. I was in so much pain that the ER staff noticed and took me for IV right after vitals.

I could finally tell a doctor what was bothering me without consequences. Nobody at home would beat me. I told her my entire past and how I never got any tests done. She asked me to wait outside while they got some ready. At least the IV was helping.

"Riya."

Anaya and I both looked up to see Vihaan.

"What're you doing here?" I asked.

"Varun called me, crying. He told me you were headed here with Anaya, so I ran over to make sure you were okay."

Crying? My husband was crying? He was always happy. We called him our golden retriever.

"I'll get you some water," Anaya said and left.

Okay, what the hell was happening with these two?

"You okay?" Vihaan asked me.

I nodded and told him what was going on. He seemed to understand why I had to bring Anaya. He wasn't upset about it, but I knew from the look he was thinking about what she went through.

"Question is, are you okay?" I asked.

"I'm not the one sitting with an IV."

"What's happening between you two?" I clarified.

"She wants to move back to the West Coast. I told her she didn't need to work, but she won't listen. I'm scared we're going to break up. I love her, Riya. I love her so much. It scares me that she won't be around anymore."

"She loves you too. A lot. Trust me, I've heard the way she talks about you. I'll fly to Oregon and kick her ass if she does anything."

We didn't say another word on that subject as Anaya came back.

I got called back about fifteen minutes later. I asked them to come with me because I was so scared. I was thankful to be surrounded by friends that cared so much about me.

The doctor ran some tests as she asked some questions. I'd be uncomfortable answering these in front of another man. Vihaan was more like a brother than a friend to me, always showing up whenever Varun or I needed him.

The doctor studied everything before coming to the conclusion of fibroids. I did have heavy periods, so I was not surprised. It was what Varun had suspected at some point. I decided to ask the doctor about the surgical procedure that my husband had suggested.

"We can if you don't want kids. I say that since it may cause complications. The safest option is a hysterectomy," the doctor said.

I saw how Vihaan looked at Anaya when the doctor said that. I wasn't selfish enough to think, 'Why did he do that? I'm the one in pain.'

"I need to call my husband," I said. "I want to have this conversation before I agree to anything."

Anaya and Vihaan asked if I wanted to speak in private. I didn't, but here was a chance to get them two alone, so I said yes.

Varun didn't pick up the first time. He probably got busy again. I tried again, and he answered right away this time.

"Hi, princess."

"I can't believe you cried!" That wasn't the first thing that was supposed to leave my mouth, but it did.

"Fucking Vihaan! He had one job."

That made me chuckle. I used my time wisely since he was probably busy. I told him everything that was going on, and he said he was okay with taking the safest way out.

"Like I said, you are more important than anything. Don't wait for me to be there. I'd love to be, but I'm okay with you feeling better. I spoke to the person in charge, and we rescheduled my flight. I'll be home tomorrow evening. If that's where you'll be, I'll come straight to the hospital."

"You did that for me?"

"Yes. I'm sorry we couldn't find one for earlier."

"I love you! See you tomorrow! Muah!"

He laughed. "I want a real kiss when I see you tomorrow. I have to go back to this meeting. I love you more."

I let him go back and told the doctor I'd take the safest option. My friends are by my side now, and my husband will be here tomorrow.

I had the doctor provide me some information. We couldn't do it right away. However, since I was in an insane amount of pain, I asked for the evening or night. She had to make calls, research, and prepare for me, but she could not find someone for the evening. Until then, I was to get myself mentally and physically ready for this. They handled most of the other stuff. It was the mental stuff I needed to operate.

I told Vihaan and Anaya to go home. They both refused. It seemed they worked everything out from their closeness. See, sometimes you have to kick people out for them to understand.

The evening rolled around slowly. We didn't have much to do in this room anyways. I was just told I'd be sleeping throughout the procedure. Worked for me because I slept through that and then through the night. Well, as best as I could anyways. I needed pain medication!

Anaya had dropped off some clothes and toiletries when she came to check back up on me. Vihaan was closer to this hospital, so they told me I could call them if I needed anything. Anaya would sleep over there tonight.

The following morning the doctor came back to check up on me. She was honestly one of the sweetest people. She informed me I'd be staying for five days, and since this was a major surgery, it could take up to eight weeks to recover. I wished Anaya had seen this doctor instead of the one that took Amber's money to turn Anaya's life upside down.

"Come in," I said as someone I assumed was a nurse, considering how early it was, knocked on the door.

To my surprise, my husband walked in with a bouquet of beautiful flowers. I tried to sit up to greet him but couldn't.

"You said evening!"

"It's called a surprise." He smiled as he kissed my forehead. "I missed you. I'm so proud of you for making this decision for yourself. I'll be here now for . . . How many days are you stuck here?"

"Five, and thank you. I missed you too."

He took my hand in his as he kissed it softly. "How's the pain?" he asked.

"Horrible! It's going to take some time to recover."

"Do you want anything to eat or drink?"

"No. Just sit here with me."

"Will do."

I wondered how my in-laws would react to this. What if they started to hate me? I knew many stories of women tortured for choosing their well-being over having to give the family a kid. It was not just in the brown community but almost everywhere.

"What're you thinking about?" Varun asked.

I shook my head. "Nothing. Just some pain, but it's not as bad as having to deal with being abused for almost thirty years. At least this one comes with a deadline and recovery time. Abuse leaves a horrible scar because you think it's done, yet you still have nightmares about it."

He looked at me, puzzled. "You have nightmares about the abuse? Why didn't you ever tell me?"

Shit! I meant to keep that to myself. Why did I say it aloud?

"Ummm, no. I don't."

"Riya," he said in a tone that told me he figured it out.

"You win. I still have nightmares and wish they'd deport themselves out of my life."

"Riya, nightmares are the brain's way of coping with trauma. We can speak with a therapist if you want. It'll be beneficial for you to discuss everything with them."

Guess I was going to therapy. I was already looking forward to getting the help I needed. Therapy was never a bad thing. I needed to look into it while I was going to be on bed rest for the next few weeks. I was going to tell him what I had planned to do when someone else knocked on the door. I thought again it could be medical staff or my friends, but this time it was my in-laws.

"Riya, how are you feeling? We found out you were in the hospital and drove back right that second," my mother-in-law said.

"I'm okay. Nothing major. Ha-ha."

I have three people now looking at me like I was on drugs. Technically, I was.

"You're being weird," my husband said. "Is it time for some medicine or something?"

I'd come to the conclusion that I didn't like this man.

"Riya, we know what happened. If you're worried that we're mad or upset about anything, we are not. Not only saying it because you're in the hospital but because you are our daughter first and daughter-in-law second. Varun told us everything before he flew over," my father-in-law said.

"But don't you both want to be grandparents? Didn't my health take that away from you?"

"Nope. It's more selfish of someone to want something that could bring others pain. I just want you both to be married for a long time," my mother-in-law said as she took my hand. "You let us know if you need anything. We're all here for you."

She wasn't kidding with the use of the word *all*. Vihaan showed up about ten seconds later with bowls full of food.

"When the hell did you get here?" he asked his best friend.

"This morning. You did all this? That's a lot of food."

"She's my friend, so I had to. Anaya and I woke up at 4:00 a.m. to get started because hospital food sucks. She fell asleep while waiting for the salmon to finish cooking." Vihaan turned to me. "I'm going to apologize for not waking her up again. She's not a morning person, very moody if you wake her up. She had no problem waking up to help cook, but I was scared to wake her up again."

"It's okay, Vihaan. I really appreciate having everyone by my side. You should get going since you have to open the restaurant soon. I'm happy to have protein served from Veg Spice Café though." I laughed.

Vihaan's restaurant specialized in vegetarian meals, but he did his research. Protein was supposed to help me recover. It was about to be my breakfast, lunch, and dinner.

He left with my in-laws, and I was alone with my husband. Varun had helped me sit up and offered to feed me. I didn't mind the intimacy, so I let him. Plus, I really missed him.

"Did you eat?" I asked when it occurred to me that he probably hadn't.

"You eat first. I'll eat what you don't."

"So you haven't had breakfast?"

"I had food on the plane. I'm okay, princess. I'll have what you don't."

I did need to eat. I would have told him I was full right then and there if I didn't. Instead, I took his hand as he was about to feed me my next bite and told him to eat. He had to have something.

Once done with breakfast and after the medical staff had checked up on me, Varun and I went back to talking before I got sleepy.

"I'll be right here or actually over there when you wake up. Get some rest, my strong angel," he said, pointing to the tiny space by the window.

He kissed my hand again before kissing my forehead.

"I thought I was your princess," I pouted.

"Whatever you are, you're mine, and you are strong. I love you."

"I love you too. Thanks for flying back for me and being by my side."

"I'd do anything for you."

That I knew he would.

Chapter 7

The recovery period was painful. I felt that when I'd die, I could sum half of my life as painful.

All I could do was lie down or do light work around the house. I couldn't go shopping alone since I couldn't carry heavy bags. I couldn't work out until after six weeks. I couldn't be in a car until the incision was healing without a problem. Why did women have to go through all the pain? Men existed!

Varun was nothing but patient with me. All my whining, complaining, and bitching, he listened to it all. He took care of me all day before I sent him packing back to work.

My mother-in-law was the one taking care of me while Varun was out. Ash was busy, but even if he had one second only, he'd come to check in on me. My father-in-law was in the same boat.

"I'm home!" Varun sang as he walked in.

"You're early," I said, glancing at the clock.

"For you. I skipped lunch and asked to have appointments bumped so I could come home to you. Don't worry. My employees still got their lunch break," he said, kissing my forehead and working his way down to my nose and then my lips.

Unfair! I had to wait because of this surgery. I didn't want to want anymore. I missed our passionate kisses. He only did soft ones because he was aware we couldn't do anything until okayed by the doctor.

I didn't want to wait. I pulled him back and kissed him. I was taking control now. I went as deep as I could with the kiss.

"Riya," he said, pulling away, "we can't. You know we can't. I need your safety and healing above anything. I can wait. I'm in no rush, princess."

Yes, but the last time we did anything was the night before he went to Sweden. It'd been almost six weeks. I wished I had hit the six-week mark, but I had to go based on the doctor's order.

We could still make out though, couldn't we? It wasn't anything more, so I decided that was what I would do.

"My eyes!" We heard Ash scream in horror as we quickly pulled away. He'd seen us kissing so much I was sure we scarred the guy.

"What're you doing here?" Varun asked.

"I came to see if *bhabi* needed anything. I was taking a study break. Didn't think you'd be home already."

Varun frowned. I was sure he thought he wouldn't be coming home early tomorrow.

"Well, I see she doesn't need me, so I'll go back to studying," Ash quickly said before literally running away.

I slapped my husband's arm. "You didn't close the door?"

"I didn't because I thought I would just put my stuff down and grab you something to eat. It's what I usually do," he defended.

"We probably have him never wanting to watch a movie with a kiss scene," I joked.

"True. At least we were only kissing."

That sentence made me think about how patient he was at the start.

★★★

A year into our wedding, but still nothing. I shouldn't feel this way. Was it trauma holding me back? I was never abused in that sense. Why am I so scared?

My body was covered in scars. I kept my entire body covered to the best of my ability. I was always self-conscious. I know I had shown my scars to Vihaan and Anaya, but when I started going out for interviews, I hated the way people looked at me. I began to cover up again.

Varun had just come home from work. It was two past our first anniversary. I thought he hated me because we didn't go further in a year.

"You okay? Did someone say something?" he asked as I realized I was sitting very still.

I nodded before shaking my head. Honesty was going to be a key component of our relationship.

I asked if he hated me for not being ready to go forward.

"Me? Hate you? That's impossible. Take your time," he replied.

"I'm just worried that you might think I'm ugly when you see me without anything. There are only a select few places where I don't have scars. I went back to full sleeves because everyone else always stares, and they dismiss me."

He took my hand in his. "Riya, I've seen your scars. Both internal and external. Not all of them, but I know you're beautiful. That won't ever change. You are beautiful.

Every scar you have tells a story. I'd rather listen to those than rush you into something."

He knew a lot of the stories behind my scars. None of them were self-given scars. Each received my brothers, mom, dad, or a combination of the three. He was there when I'd tell Vihaan and Anaya. I didn't want to repeat it, so I'd tell the three of them together.

"It's just that we've been married for a year. I remember back in college, some guy left a girl because she wouldn't give in to him after a month of being together. I'm scared," I told him.

"First, if a guy keeps telling a girl or his partner anything to the point they have to give in unwillingly, that's abuse. Report it. Second, we have been together for over a month. I'd never walk out on you. Third, I understand why you'd be scared. I'm staying forever. I'd never do anything without your permission."

That was true. Sometimes he'd even ask me for permission to hang out with Vihaan. I wonder why he thought he'd need permission for that. He even asked me if it was okay to give me back hugs since he wanted consent for anything that required physical contact.

"I know. I'm sorry for bringing this up," I said.

"No, you don't ever apologize for anything. You have no need to apologize, princess. Got it?"

I nodded as I rolled my pants up from the ankle.

"Have you seen this one?" I questioned.

"Yes. I don't know the story behind it."

"This was because I tried to leave the house. The popular kid invited me to a party. Of course, I had to go! I tried to sneak out when I thought everyone was busy. Got caught and beat with a kendo stick. My mom's goal was to break my foot off so I couldn't go anywhere. The neighbors saw everything that day and threatened to call Child Protection Services. My parents gave them about $4,000 and told them to keep quiet."

He leaned down to kiss the scar. I wasn't expecting that at all. It felt strange but a good kind of strange.

"I want you to think of me as a balm. It's what makes wounds better, right? I'll be your balm."

★★★

Varun was snapping his fingers in front of me, bringing me back to the present moment. He really had to ruin the flashback I was having. Rude, but I loved him, so I'd let it slide.

I grabbed his hand to make him stop snapping.

"Welcome back to reality. The year is . . ."

I cut him off. "Shut up. I know the year. I was thinking about something."

"After making out? At least it's something, not someone."

I gave him a look that I always did when I wanted him to think about what he said.

"You know I'm still very sorry about that. I still live by the words that I'll spend my life making it up to you," he said right away.

I didn't say anything. I kissed him again, not caring we didn't close the door yet.

"You really are my balm. I love you," I said, pulling away.

"I love you too, princess."

Varun

Chapter 8

Something happened. Not the surgery but something else. She was hiding something and seemed to always be on edge. I'd tried asking her about it multiple times, but I had had no luck. Riya quickly dismissed the question, saying it was just her pain.

I wanted to stay home with her while she recovered, but she pushed me into going to work. I'd probably go back to staring at my phone, waiting for an update like I did when she went to her cousin's wedding.

"You have someone that would like to see you," Angela said.

I really hated that both of my assistants' names were almost identical. One was Angie, and the other was Angela. I questioned why I did that to myself every single day. I could almost guarantee I was probably stressed about Riya when I made the decision. She'd been the only thing on my mind since we first met.

"Now? I have appointments," I said.

"She says it's crucial."

"Is it Riya?" I asked.

"No."

"Anaya? Esha?" I questioned.

"No. Her name is . . ."

I cut her off. "Then it's not important. She can wait."

Why did I even ask if it was Esha? She didn't leave the house. The priority list started with Riya, my mom, and Vihaan's girlfriend and sister. I could find nobody else important enough to push past appointment times for.

I dismissed Angela and went to see my next patient, a teenager who was getting used to contact lenses. People did have a hard time getting used to them at first. I went over the usual exam process, which was the easy part. It was always the question(s) that took more time.

"Due to being in front of a computer all day, I wish to return to glasses. Computer vision syndrome, ya know, Doc?"

Teens! I sighed.

"Yes, I know. There are lenses made especially for that. I'll tell my assistant to help you out. Do you have other questions?"

She shook her head, and I told Angie to set her up with lenses instead of contacts.

I should check in on Riya before I go to my next patient. I was typing away when Angela told me the next patient had to cancel due to an emergency.

Well, that gave me until after lunch for the next one. I should text Riya before I told Angela to bring in whoever was waiting.

VARUN: Hi princess 👸 how are you feeling?

RIYA: Did you just use the princess emoji? 1st time!

RIYA: I'm good. The meds help. Anaya is here to help make sure I don't die of boredom. How's work? Make any friends? Or did you chase away the ones you have?

VARUN: OK. 1st of all I have 1 best friend. 2nd I have no friends at work. 3rd I did use the emoji. 4th, that's sweet of Anaya.

RIYA: Shouldn't you be with a patient?

VARUN: They canceled.

RIYA: 👁🌊

RIYA: Get it? I see 🤣

VARUN: I got it, princess. Have fun with Anaya. I have someone here to see me

RIYA: Bye. Love you 💚

VARUN: I love you too, my strong angel 😇

I called the reception area to let Angela know they could come in. I decided to work on organizing some files while they showed up.

I almost dropped everything when I saw who it was. I'm sure if I had a mirror, I'd be seeing my face as pale as these envelopes I was getting ready.

"You have no right to be here," I snarled.

Camren had no business being anywhere near me or my wife again. Was this why Riya had been on edge? Camren was supposed to have left with Amber for England.

"How was your trip?" she asked.

"What trip? I didn't go on a trip," I lied.

Who the fuck told Camren I was out of the country?

"The trip to Sweden," she smirked.

What the fuck?

Why did Camren even know that? Did she have people watching me? Was she that desperate?

"Listen, I didn't go on a trip. If you don't disappear in the next two seconds, I will have you lovingly escorted by the police."

The cops must have memorized my place by now.

She came closer instead. "How about a kiss? For old times' sake."

I pushed her away—physically pushed her.

"You mean the biggest regret of my life? You. You were and will always be the biggest regret I have. Get out of here, Camren. You are currently in violation of a restraining order."

I'd be dumb not to immediately get restraining orders against Camren and Amber.

"I'm leaving. Just make sure your wife stays alive," she said as if she was the villain in a horror film who guessed what happened next.

She left immediately after saying that. I'd check with Riya. I'd go through her phone because Riya's safety was my priority.

The workday went by after lunch as if a snail was moving the arrows on the clock. It was going as fast as a cheetah before that.

'Fuck Camren!' Those were the two words I had texted Vihaan when I was so angry I thought I'd break something. He was now calling me.

"Tell me what happened. There's no way you texted me that to just say it," he said concerned.

"She showed up here." I told him everything from the trip to her threat.

"Riya's safely at home. Breathe. She's okay and safe. You have one appointment left, since I learned you take about thirty minutes per patient. You'll go home and see she's safe," he reassured me. "Take some deep breaths."

I did. I had to calm myself down before I seemed unprofessional. I stayed on the phone until my last appointment arrived. I didn't rush it, but I only took part of the half hour.

I organized everything in my office, let the assistants go early, locked up, and sped home, sighing in relief as soon as I saw Anaya's car still parked when I arrived home.

I went upstairs to our room. Normally, Riya would run over to hug me, but these days I was the one going to her.

"I'll leave you two alone now. I'm working the evening shift part-time today," Anaya said. "Take care of her, or I will personally kill you."

I laughed at her threat. "Of course I will."

When Anaya left, I checked on Riya, asking if she had eaten, had her medication, and had her pain level. I didn't hide anything from my wife, so when she told me everything was good, I informed her about Camren's visit and what Camren told me.

"I'm safe, Varun. I'm in one piece in front of you, and I have several weeks that I can't leave the house anyways. We love being on bed rest." She smiled as she added the last part.

"I'm worried because something has been bothering you and you won't tell me the truth."

"I would have told you if it wasn't the pain. I love you, hubby. I'm excellent. If you're worried, you can put a security camera in our room."

"I'll put them all around the house," I said, leaning in for a kiss. "I love you, my strong angel."

"You know," she sighed, "I miss being called only princess."

She really did have too much time on her hands. I rolled my eyes at what she said.

"I love you, princess."

"See, much better. Let's keep it that way."

To tease her, I said, "Okay, my strong angel. We'll keep it that way."

"You really are an asshole. Vihaan's correct."

Vihaan's ego would skyrocket when I told him that. Now, that was something I couldn't wait to see. I should be fine if they weren't in the same place when I told him.

Chapter 9

I COULD LEAVE THE BED! THAT FELT LIKE FOREVER, BUT NOW I could move around! I was so excited. Not the going back to work part, but everything else. Work sucked! I couldn't believe I wanted to work more than anything else. What was I thinking? I hated it!

I wouldn't quit though. Not yet, at least, because I had to build my résumé. I had gone to work for a week before calling out sick today since I hated my job.

Varun had half-day Fridays now, so he'd be home early today! I was so excited since Fridays meant going to a movie or shopping. I loved spending time with my husband even more now that I could finally get off this bed. Remember to make the most of life because you never know when it will be put on pause again.

It was 11:54 a.m. right now, which meant it would be around 12:30 p.m. to 12:45 p.m., depending on traffic, when he'd be home. I should start doing my makeup right now in that case.

My phone's ringtone made me jump as I took the makeup out of the vanity. I wanted to try the smoky eye look today.

"Hi, Anaya!" I happily greeted.

"Hey, are you busy?" she asked with a sense of urgency.

"Nope. What happened? Do you need me to come over?" I asked, putting my brush down.

"No, it's nothing serious. I was just bored at work. Vihaan's busy, so I thought I'd call you," she said.

Well, I could start my makeup while we chatted away. I'd have given her my full attention if it was an important topic, but she was just complaining about work. She knew how much I hated working too. In fact, I was the one who texted her that I had taken today off.

It wasn't a long phone call. She had a ten-minute break, which was over after she vented about how much she also hated her job.

I finished my makeup, and I was impressed. For someone doing a smokey eye look for the first time, I liked it. I threw on a white jumper and orange joggers since I wanted to be comfortable, but I realized that my makeup didn't match now. I was not changing anything. I'd go out like a clown instead.

I sent Varun a text asking when he was coming home.

Varun: It's Thursday

Riya: No, it's Friday

Varun: Oh wait you're right. Idk how I forgot. Been so busy

Riya: It happens.

Varun: No wonder Vihaan asked if I'm popping up at the restaurant ☠

Varun: I'll be over soon, princess. I love you!

Riya: I love you too. Can we go to the movies?

Varun: Anything you want 😍

I put my phone back down. All I had to do now was wait. I blocked the number that had sent me those baleful text messages. When Varun came home and told me about Camren revisiting him, I felt it was her doing. I still couldn't believe that bitch took advantage of his past feelings for her and blackmailed him into everything he did to Anaya and Vihaan. She wanted to be with him so desperately that she was trying to threaten me? Had she seen a mirror? She thought Varun would leave me for her. The audacity of that bitch.

I still wouldn't tell him about the text messages because he'd freak out more than he did about safety as it was. I preferred to not be watched 24-7 anymore. He would put security everywhere.

I did want to casually bring it up before we headed out. I was lucky I emailed the text messages and number to myself. If Varun went through my phone, he wouldn't find the text since they were deleted and the email address I used was one I always logged out of.

"I'm home!" Varun said, walking in.

"I have eyes. I can see that," I replied.

"Damn! What did I do to deserve the sass?"

I rolled my eyes. It wasn't meant to be sassy or lead us into this steamy kiss that was now happening between us. I missed this so much! How dare he pull away? Did he not realize how much I missed him? Jerk.

"How was your day?" he asked. "I love your eye makeup by the way. I love you in general, so anything you do is perfect. You're perfect."

Was I not blushing enough from that kiss? Why did I feel my cheeks heat up again?

"I didn't do anything," I replied. "And thank you."

I loved how he looked at me as if I were the only woman in the world. I'd caught him looking at me like that on several occasions. When we went out and he went to the guys while I went to the girls, his eyes were always searching for me. I low-key thought it was for safety but later realized it was not just that.

"I want to ask you something," I said, purposely moving my phone to the side but not out of reach.

"Anything."

"What would you do if someone tried to threaten me?" I asked without saying anything about the text. "And don't say security cameras."

"Is that why you've been so worked up? Did something happen? Camren did say—"

"Nothing happened. I was watching a true crime documentary and got curious," I lied.

Varun grabbed my phone before I could stop him and went through my text. That wasn't going to help him.

"You won't find anything in there."

He put the phone away. "Riya, I love you. I say this way too often, but your safety is my number one priority. If anyone even touched a hair on you, I'd have their body delivered to their family in a casket."

"Well, caskets cost a lot of money, so you're technically doing them a favor," I said with my lip curving about a quarter upwards, hinting I was attempting a joke.

"Hilarious," he said without laughing. "Your safety isn't a joke to me. I won't be like your family who kept you locked up, but I will want to know if you feel anything fishy is happening. Promise you'll tell me."

"I promise, husband," I said, giving him a peck. "Can we go to the movies now?"

He nodded and left to change into something a little more casual. I texted Vihaan from my end that we'd drop by after watching a movie and I was in the mood for some noodles. He really is one of my best friends because he replied with, 'I don't need to be a Michelin star chef to make you noodles. Order something from the menu Riya.'

R- I'm telling Anaya

V- rude. You can't use my girlfriend against me

R- why not? She's my best friend.

V- ...

R- I'll take that as a yes

V - I'm making cheap noodles for you both bc I can guarantee my best friend put you up to this. Store-bought 🍜

R- he didn't. I was the one wanting them. I'll tell Anaya you don't want to

V- OK. Only because you're using my girlfriend against me. Not nice ☹️ Varun is rubbing off you 😭 sad times truly.

I couldn't stop laughing at the last message he wrote. I had to take a few deep breaths to calm myself down while Varun came back. I showed him the phone, to which he rolled his eyes.

On the drive to the theater, I asked Varun about his day. He always had the same response, "Same shit. Different day."

"I wish my shit paid as well as yours did."

"Princess, you don't need to work. We've been over this an ample amount of times."

If we've been over it so many times, why did it not register to him that I wish to work. I just need to build a resume. I decided simply to not answer back to that as we pulled into a gas station about halfway through our drive. We wanted to go to the cinema with the recliners, which meant another forty-minute drive. At least it's Saturday tomorrow.

While Varun was pumping gas I looked around mindlessly until my eyes landed on a woman who seemed to be getting abused by her partner, if that was her partner. It could be a different relationship.

I didn't even think twice before I pulled out my phone and called the police. There's no way in hell I'm going to let someone be abused and watch it happen, nor was I going to film it for the gram as some people do.

Once I got word the police were on their way and Varun barely opened his door, I opened mine, leaving everything I owned in the car to run to that woman.

"Hey! There you are. We've been waiting to go to the movies together," I said, pretending to know her. I have to get her out of this situation in any way possible. I turned to the guy. "Have we met before?"

He shook his head. That's right! You better act calm because if you even lay a finger on me, Varun will have your family planning a funeral.

I turned my attention back to the woman, who seemed to calm down, knowing someone was there.

"What happened? Where did you go? Should we head back?" I asked.

The police showed up right then and there, surrounding the area so he couldn't run away. They handcuffed him and threw him in the back. I gave my witness story and patiently waited for the girl to tell hers.

She wouldn't stop thanking me after everything was cleared. I offered to buy her a warm meal, even though I didn't know exactly what would be a warm meal from a gas station.

"I know. I saw everything and I'm so proud of you," Varun said when I opened the door to explain and grab my purse.

"I want to buy her a warm meal and ensure she safely gets home."

"You won't find a warm meal here. Tell her to join us. We'll take her for one," he replied and I nodded.

I'm so in love with my husband.

We learned the woman's name was Riley. She told us that she was thrown into this marriage because her dad had a gambling addiction and bet her off. It was a very abusive marriage from the start. He had hurt her in public multiple times, but people only ever recorded it for clout in the day and age of Tiktok. Today was the first time someone stepped in and helped.

I was the first person to ever help! Wow! A few years back, I wouldn't even be able to help myself. This confidence came from being married to Varun. Typically, seeing someone else being abused would've turned me into a track star running in the opposite direction but not anymore.

Varun pulled up to Vihaan's restaurant and explained the situation. Vihaan was happy to help serve her a warm meal and even some dessert.

We never dined out with everyone else. We would always have a special place inside the kitchen for ourselves since his kitchen was ginormous.

I paid Vihaan for the meal on her behalf, but he didn't take the payment. Told us it was on the house instead.

I said just to mess with him, "Anaya's rubbing off on you."

"Please. I barely ever see her. I kiss her," he said. "Miss! Fuck! Miss! I miss her! I really do fucking miss her. Tell your best friend to make some time for me."

I shouldn't laugh but I couldn't help it.

"I'm sure that's what you meant," I teased.

"I wish I could kiss her," he pouted.

"I'll let her know. She's always working."

"I know. It sucks! She doesn't have to work, Riya. I'll do all the money-making. She could sit at home and read books all day for all I care. I just want to spend time with her and not have conflicting schedules. I miss her so much."

Does Anaya even read? I don't remember. But seeing Vihaan in this condition just because he can't see her, imagine if they broke up. He'd lose himself. It's a good thing they love each other too much for a breakup to even happen.

Varun

Chapter 10

I wouldn't say I hate family gatherings, but I'm sure there are other things I could be doing.

We were at my cousin's house for his birthday. I could care less about him. I didn't like him, but I fully displayed my fakeness, pretending I was happy to be there.

"Bro, your wife have a sister or something? Maybe a cousin I could get with?" He asked.

El, as we called him, was known to be a player because he didn't like his name. Point proven. This is why I don't like him.

"She only has three brothers. I can hook you up if you'd like," I told him. They'd get along great. They're all assholes anyway.

"Sorry. I don't swing that way."

He went back to wherever he came from before annoying me. Even if Riya had some female in her life, I would never risk that woman's life. I know my cousin. Never!

I followed him after a few seconds. My gut instinct told me I should and you should always listen to your gut.

He began to check Riya out. Thankfully he sees me tomorrow for his eye exam. I know exactly how to make him go blind.

"Riya," I said, getting her attention within the crowd of people.

She looked towards me as I motioned for her to come here. She gracefully walked towards me, but El kept his eyes on her. He's definitely going to be blind tomorrow.

"We're leaving. Get your things," I told her, keeping my voice stern.

"Thank God! I was so bored!"

Two birds one stone.

On the drive home, I informed Riya that she was being checked out by my cousin. Her reply was that she had noticed it but stayed silent to not create a scene.

I had let my assistants go home before the final appointment since it was the final one, but also because I didn't need them here to be witnesses.

"Thanks for doing this. Your wife has such a, how do I say this without being rude, hot body! But anyways, we're here to talk about my eyes. Nice to have a doctor in the family."

I'm going to put him in the emergency room and pray he doesn't make it.

"Of course," I faked a smile. "What's family for?"

I got to work on all the usual exam questions and procedures.

"Wait, read that bottom line again," I told him.

He read it missing two letters, so I told him to try again.

"Hmmm. I have some drops that might work. Let me put those in right now and then we'll try again. It may burn a bit," I grinned, knowing he couldn't see that.

I put three drops of the special medicine I made for him in each eye.

"It does burn! A lot!" He complained.

"Give it a minute. Try rereading it."

He hissed in pain. "I can't! It burns! Take me to the eye wash!"

Over my dead body. "We don't have one."

"How do you not have one? You're an eye doctor!"

He doesn't even know the proper term for my profession. What was I going to expect from a man who was spoiled by his mother? No wonder he gets away with what he does.

"You should go to the ER. I have another patient," I lied. "Maybe someone can take you."

It would be too late by the time anyone came.

"I can't get to my phone! Call my mom!" He barked.

I don't do disrespect. "Here, take my hand. I'll help you."

He grabbed my hand and I walked him out of the building, locking the door. He kept banging on it, but she should have thought about that before looking at Riya the way he did.

I went back to my office, turned the music up, finished any paperwork and took the back exit. I was wise to park there today.

When I got home, I went to see Riya, who wasn't there. Strange, she's usually home before me. I searched around until Ash said she stepped out to see Anaya. Alright then, what do I do? My phone went off and answered that. Looks like I'm chatting with the group.

Procrastination Station 🚉

R- *photo*

R- *photo*

A- *photo*

VIHAAN- You went clubbing?!

A- esy

R- she's drunk. We got off early. Decided why not?

VIHAAN- she's an annoying drunk

A- you're an annoying boyfriend 🙄

VARUN- at least she spelled that correctly 🤣

R- not now 🙈

A- Vihaan. Cimw safe me

R- she means come save me

VIHAAN- I'm working 😑 and who told her to go clubbing?

A- need a new boyfriend

VARUN- I love how she's spelling all the insults correctly.

R - stop ✋

A- Vihaan diswnt lub me

R- doesn't love me*

VIHAAN- I'd give my own life up for you!

R- she's crying in the club! Saying you don't love her

VIHAAN- 🙄🙄🙄🙄🙄

VARUN- should I come get you both?

A- no. Bigdrind clme get me

R- sigh. No boyfriend come get me*

A- Varun get Riya

R- I'm not leaving her drunk ass here!

R- I have to go. This guy keeps trying to make moves on Anaya.

VIHAAN- I'm coming. Text me your location. Tell security there's about to be a fight.

A - he teied to kss ma

R- he tried to kiss me* Anaya, where'd you go? You were with me a second ago.

R- Vihaan *location attached*

A- voyfend restaurant. 🚶

R- Vihaan hurry please! She walked out and the guy was following her.

Well, I don't have anything better to do. I grabbed my keys to help my friends out and ran out the door. If Anaya was headed to see Vihaan from that club, I should take exit 5. I'll find her easier that way. I roamed the streets, praying to find someone. Riya called me to say Vihaan got her, but they can't find Anaya. I told her I was looking as well. She was panicking so much as Vihaan and I tried to calm her down.

This wasn't her fault. It wasn't anyone's fault except the alcohol.

I began to circle the areas where she could possibly be. Thankfully, the girls sent us photos of them, so I knew what she'd be wearing.

Bingo! I sped a bit to get to her. I pulled over where I could. Why is the red so annoyingly long?

"Anaya," I said, getting her attention. "Let's get you home."

"No! You tried to kill me."

That wasn't untrue. I never wanted to hurt her. Camren blackmailed me into everything I did.

"Anaya, I'm not going to hurt you. Please, let's go home."

"Vihaan," she said.

"He'll meet us there. Look, you're very drunk. You can't even stand, so please."

I started to draw the attention of a few people passing by. They probably think I'm taking advantage when I want to get my future sister-in-law back into my best friend's embrace.

"Anaya, people are watching."

She looked around when I told her.

"Promise?" She asked.

Promise what? Fuck it! Anything to get her safely to Vihaan. "Yes."

I helped her to the car and to sit down. On the drive back, she began to sob. I have no idea where that came from. "He soesn lub me."

Where's Riya? I think she said he doesn't love me.

"Vihaan loves you more than anything in this world. Ask for anything, and he'll give it to you."

"Why won't he marry me?"

You know I have that same question. They've been together since before Riya and I got married, so why hasn't he proposed. I'll have to knock some sense into him.

"He will, Anaya. Even if he has to elope, he doesn't want anyone else to be his wife. Not to brag, but I've known Vihaan long enough to know he's crazy about you regardless of how he behaves."

"That was a brag!"

I pulled up to my house where Vihaan's and... is that my aunt's car?

"Don't tell Vihaan anything," Anaya said.

"Oh, trust me. I think there's a whole other conversation waiting for me inside," I said as she looked at me. "I won't tell him. Promise."

I got out of my side, running around to help Anaya out. I thought Vihaan said she's annoying when drunk. She definitely wasn't irritating. A little stubborn, though. Their kids will get the stubbornness gene....oh wait. Shit! I forgot about that. Thankfully, I didn't say it aloud.

I opened the door to find everyone. Vihaan pulled me aside to let me know he was going to take her home and Riya was still in shock. He thanked me for bringing her before leaving.

"Where's Riya?" I asked.

"Upstairs," mom answered. I turned to go, but mom said I was needed here."

I knew it! Alright, let's get this over with.

"See! Look at him bringing other women home!" My aunt looked at me like I had committed a crime.

"Anaya is Riya's best friend. She's also Vihaan's girlfriend, so she's not just another woman. If you want someone who brings a different woman home every night, go look at your son!"

"Varun," my mom calmly warned me before saying. "Your aunt tells me El went blind because of some medicine you gave."

So it worked! Beautiful! "Sorry, mom, but unfortunately, I have no idea what you're talking about. He did have an eye appointment with me. I did the usual exam and dismissed him."

"You forgot the eyedrops part!" My aunt barked.

"What eyedrops? Are you sure your son wasn't high on something? He does smoke, drink, and sleep around every chance he gets. Look," I pulled Instagram up from my phone. "Just look at his page."

I threw the phone at her. Such a beautiful sight exposing him and getting away with it.

"It seems my son is innocent, so I'd appreciate it if you apologized for doubting him and his character," dad said, looking over her shoulder at the phone.

"You're saying my son is a liar?" She asked him.

"Probably got it from you," I answered.

"Varun," mom warned me again.

I need her to leave. Apology or not, I want to see Riya.

My aunt began to argue with my parents. That's where she fucked up. Ash and I don't take lightly anyone raising their voice at our parents. Hell, our grandparents weren't even allowed to disrespect them.

Ash was the one who grabbed her from the sofa by the wrist and threw her out. She probably scraped her elbow the way she fell.

"Nobody speaks to my parents like that!" He yelled before closing the door and asking our parents if they're alright.

I told him I was proud of what he did.

"You rubbed off on me," he replied. "Go see bhabi. Is Anaya alright, by the way? She looked like she cried."

I couldn't tell anyone. I made a promise to her about the real reason. "She got followed by some douche from the club."

"That sucks! I'll ask Vihaan if it's okay that I offer therapy if she ever needs it. I can't believe I have two sisters-in-law! Well, one to come still. That's the best thing about having an older brother and being best friends with Vihaan."

"Hey! I'm Vihaan's best friend! Get behind me."

"Something tells me I don't have to get behind you." He stuck his tongue out and left.

I'm calling Vihaan tomorrow! They better not be having secret bro dates or something!

I checked in on Riya, who was still shaken up and crying. I sat by her, hugging her, letting her know everything was fine.

"It was my idea. I'm a horrible friend," she cried.

"Riya, it's not your fault. The alcohol got the best of her."

"I never went clubbing, so I decided a weekday should be alright. I'm so sorry. I ruined everything."

I kept hugging her. "You did nothing wrong."

"You can blame me for once!"

"No! Why would I? Anaya's with Vihaan. She's safe."

She moved so she could see my face. "Did she say anything? Did he?"

"No. Vihaan only said thanks and you were upset."

"Vihaan wasn't blaming me either. I would've felt better if he did."

This the same person that didn't want to be blamed for things since she had to deal with it growing up?

I decided it was best to simply hold her. I love her. I don't need her to feel worse. Vihaan, Anaya and myself won't blame her for anything. I'm not saying that because of her past. I'm saying it because we know Riya wasn't the one to blame.

Varun

Chapter II

THE BEST WAY TO BEAT THE HEAT, GO TO YOUR BEST FRIEND'S restaurant and get some mango lassi.

"It's not on the menu. Why do you all keep doing this to me?" He asked, frustrated.

The second option, wait for his girlfriend to arrive and beg her to ask him for it.

Mango lassi is a sweet drink made out of yogurt or curd and mangoes or mango pulp.

"Where's Riya?" Vihaan asked.

"Working. I was thirsty, so I came to bother you."

"I should not have given you a second chance to be my friend."

Anaya finally showed up and without me even asking her if she could beg him, she simply told him it was what she wanted.

"You are so lucky I'm in love with you," he told her. "So lucky."

Now we wait. Anaya came and sat over by me.

"Hey, has Riya told you weird things keep happening when she's out?" She asked, placing her phone on the table across.

What kind of weird? Why is Riya hiding something from me?

"No. It's not like her to hide anything."

"Strange. She usually tells you everything. Maybe she doesn't want you to have an obsession with worrying for her again."

I'm always worried about her!

Vihaan placed our drinks in front of us. "I swear to God, if you ever order anything not on the menu again, I'm banning you from the restaurant."

Anaya pretended to be hurt. "You'd ban me from seeing you?"

"Not you, beautiful. You can have whatever you want. I'm talking about him. This was his idea, wasn't it?"

I gasped. "I'm so offended."

"Ask me if I care," Vihaan said before returning to the customer's orders.

Anaya circled back to the conversation about Riya. Did it have something to do with Camren?

"Vihaan," she said to get his attention, but he was busy talking to August.

She tried again. "Chef!"

He gave her an annoyed look before coming back over. "What now?"

"I wanted to tell you I ran into Amber on the way," she said.

"I hope you rearranged her face," Vihaan said.

If Camren was here and Amber's here too, have they targeted Riya?

I told the others about my run-in with Camren the other day and the conversation I had with Riya afterward.

"Ha! She agreed with me! You are an asshole!"

Anaya gave Vihaan one look for less than five seconds and he was immediately apologizing. She has him wrapped around her finger.

"Sorry about him. He doesn't understand timing," she stated. "But that means we all need to keep an eye on her. I'm going back soon. I have only two days left here."

"I'm not having this conversation," Vihaan said and walked away.

"Sorry about him again. He can't handle the fact I'm going back home. He's making it unnecessarily hard, but this isn't about us. I noticed how it's usually one person. A male. Do you think Camren or Amber hired him?"

A male? That seems like something they'd do. I want Riya to tell me on her own. I trust that she'll get to me. That doesn't mean I won't do anything about her safety. It means I'll pretend to not know when she's telling me. I'll have Vihaan do the same. I'm sure she already knows that Anaya knows.

"You haven't gotten the police involved yet?" I asked.

"Riya refused, saying it could be a coincidence. It's happened twice already."

It's not that, but I can't tell them. Riya once tried to tell the cops about the abuse she was facing at home. Her parents paid the cops to go back and pretend nothing had happened, so they did. I don't remember how much they paid them, but she said someone else had seen it and they delivered them too. Riya only trusts seven people. Those seven people are me, Anaya, Ash, Vihaan, my parents, her cousin whose wedding she went to, and one of her co-workers.

"I need to go home. She should be home now," I told Anaya.

"Okay."

I gathered my things. "And Anaya, Vihaan's not being difficult. He loves you more than his own life. He's probably just worried."

She smiled as she nodded her head as she understood. "Bye, Varun. I'll see when I can."

"Have a safe trip. I'll see you later."

When I got home, as I do every time, I went straight to my wife.

She didn't look like something had happened or was bothering her and I'd have believed it if Anaya wasn't the one to tell me everything. These two are almost glued at the hip when they're not working or with their partner.

"You're late," she whined as she hugged me.

"I went to Vihaan's place. Tortured him into making a drink that wasn't on the menu," I informed her, kissing her.

"You'll never stop messing with him, will you?"

I shook my head. "It helped that Anaya asked for the same thing."

She let me go. "Anaya was there? What...uumm...what... like...what did you all talk about?"

I'm going to let Riya tell me when she wishes.

"How Vihaan won't make us food that's not on the menu," I told her instead.

She seemed to have calmed down. "You both really take advantage of him being a chef. You should take food to him someday. Be a good friend."

"I can't give a Michelin star chef food that I cook. It won't compare!"

"True. You do suck at cooking."

I pretended to be offended. "I cook well. I even told Vihaan I make a nice bowl of cereal."

"Ya, because people go to his restaurant for cereal."

"He said the same thing, in the same sarcastic way!"

"Maybe he is my best friend."

At this rate, anyone could have him.

I let Riya know I'm going to take a quick shower and then I'll make dinner. She can see how amazingly talented her husband really is.

I hate to be patient with her, but she's my wife and I trust her. She will tell me soon enough.

Once I finished my shower, I threw on a comfortable pair of joggers and a t-shirt before heading downstairs.

I decided on doing naan pizza. Vihaan taught me this once and has been my favorite dish ever since.

I had Riya try it first once it was done.

"So? What's the verdict?" I asked after she had a bit.

"I take back what I said. You're a decent cook."

It's better than being awful.

"You can thank me with a kiss."

She laughed. "You just want a kiss."

"Always. That's not a lie," I said, tapping my cheek.

"Has anyone ever told you that you're annoying?" She asked.

"Yes," but I didn't stop until I got my kiss.

"I love you, Riya," I said, returning the favor.

"I love you too. Now eat with me before it gets cold."

"Yes boss."

Chapter 12

I'll pay the universe whatever it wants to stop doing this to me. I barely even got off the bed and now I'm lying here with a fever. I swear I only got three weeks of not having to be glued to a bed before getting stuck again.

Stressing over the anonymous text messages wasn't helping me feel any better. I filed the report and called my carrier, who switched my phone number. It was the hardest thing to explain to Varun why I needed a new phone number. I wish he hadn't memorized it at times.

I had taken his phone while he went to shower, switched my number and put it right back where it was. However, when he called me that day, as he did almost every day, he asked why the number was different. I never told him about the threats, just said it was because I wanted to. It's undeniable he's still suspicious.

"Why aren't you in bed?" Varun asked when I came to the kitchen.

"I'm going to leave an imprint on that bed if I spend another second there," I told him, grabbing the orange juice.

"Princess, you won't feel better if you don't rest. I'm making you some oatmeal. Did you take your medicine?

Do you need another blanket? Did everything stay down today?"

I couldn't help the smile on my face. If I didn't give Varun another chance and was still with my parents, I wouldn't have been asked questions. I'd get yelled at because I didn't scrub the toilet or do the laundry. I love my husband so much. He really is the best thing that's ever happened to me.

"I didn't vomit today," I answered. "And you just came home from work. You should rest up."

"Absolutely not. My gorgeous wife is sick. I have to take care of her."

I sighed. There's no point in arguing with someone stubborn. I wasn't going back to bed, though. He can fight me.

"Let me help you," I said as an excuse to not be sent back.

"Why would you help me when you're sick? Go sit down if you don't want to lie down."

I'll take it! As long as I'm not going to bed!

I grabbed my book and a small blanket and went to sit on the sofa. I still had some orange juice in my cup, so I was set.

I did less reading and more stealing glances at my husband, who was busy cleaning up the kitchen. We're just home today, so he's doing the housework.

"What're you reading?" He asked, wiping down the coffee table.

"Just this book," I replied.

"What's it about?"

"Hmm? Oh, uhh, nothing."

"New York Times best seller and it's about nothing. They're really giving that title out to anyone."

In my defense, I have nothing. It's better than the teens on booktok hyping a book because of one line only to find out the rest of the novel is trash. Still waiting for that to be dismantled.

He placed the bowl down. "It's still hot. Let me know if you need anything else. I'm going to do some other housework before I sit with you unless you prefer I sit with you first."

I shook my head. "Finish everything, then sit by me. I don't want you to get sick. I have a mask with me."

"I don't care about getting sick. I want to spend time with you."

Of course, you do. He kissed the top of my head before leaving to go take out the trash. He should have waited because I needed to figure out how much I could eat.

When he was doing other chores, I returned to stealing glances. He's lost weight! I'm going to force-feed him when I can get better. He still looks good, but unless he wanted to lose weight on purpose, it's not something to compliment. It's more on the worrisome side.

"Riya, am I more interesting than the book?" He asked without looking up. How did he see that? I've been so careful!

"Conceited," I said as an excuse.

He laughed, "I can feel you looking at me. I'm almost done."

No, he's conceited. That's the only answer I have and the only excuse I'm going to stick with.

I buried my face in the book and began to actually read this time. It's a lovely novel about an arranged marriage where she falls first, but he falls harder, called *Contracted Together.* She's a Kindergarten teacher and he's a CEO. She's the sun, and he's the clouds, Mr. Grumpy, but she calls him Mr. Workaholic. I love when the female character gives the male character a nickname. It reminds me of Anaya's relationship.

I had my oatmeal as I read. I was waiting for the moment they'd confess, but I'm pissed that he's sent his bodyguard to look after her instead of going himself. The main character can't admit he's in love, because his abusive mom will get the CEO title if he does. The mom made the contract and he signed it saying he's never going to fall in love and this is an arranged marriage.

"Done?" Varun asked, pointing to the oatmeal.

I closed my book, putting it to the side. I loved books with Desi representation. "Ya. I still can't eat much."

"You sure you don't want to go to another doctor?"

"Yes. I'll be fine."

He sat next to me and I let myself rest in his embrace. This is what safety feels like. Someone tell the younger version of me that there's going to be a time when I'll be taken care of while sick. I won't spend my life being abused.

I asked, "What's the best thing that happened to your life? Don't be all sappy and say it was me."

"Us," he replied without hesitation.

Of course, he'd have a way around the answer.

I opened my mouth to speak, but he beat me to it. "You can ask Vihaan. I never thought marriage was for me. He was the one who dated. I was the one who focused on school. Although, he did only date Camren before Anaya. Riya, the first time I saw you, I thought you were here visiting or something. I never thought the most beautiful woman I had laid eyes on was meant to be my wife. I couldn't shut up about you for days! I think it made Vihaan immune to being annoyed by me."

I couldn't help but laugh at that.

"Riya, you didn't just come into my life. You became my life. You are my soulmate, whether you believe it or not."

I'd be stupid to not believe it. He has a way with words that any woman would be lucky to hear. Of course, I'd have to commit a crime if he ever said that to another woman. He's only allowed to offer advice about eyes to other women, and they have to be talking to him because it's their eye appointment.

"I love you," I said.

He kissed the top of my head again. "I love you too. Always."

We fell into a comfortable silence before I asked. "So what did you tell Vihaan about me besides my looks?"

"I don't know. I always spoke about how beautiful you were mostly. I mentioned your personality, but I believe most of the time I was telling him how he's never going to find anyone as beautiful as you."

I teased, "That went against you. Didn't it?"

Anaya has to be one of the most stunning women in the world. She can pass as a model for all I know.

"No, it didn't. There's nobody on this earth that is prettier than you."

I smiled to myself. "I'm telling Anaya."

"I'm sure she'll agree," he responded.

I laughed. "So you're saying Anaya isn't pretty? That's my best friend."

I faced him as he said, "I didn't say that. I said she's not as pretty as you. Vihaan would murder me if I said Anaya wasn't pretty, so he's lucky she is. Too bad I was right and got the prettiest woman on the planet to myself."

I shook my head in disbelief laughing. Yep, definitely can't do anything about how stubborn he is.

Varun

Chapter 13

Ring the doorbell one more time and I swear to God, I'm going to yell at whoever is there.

"Ash! You're so dead!" I said, going past him.

He was walking around in his room, which is closer to the stairs, so he should be the one to go answer it.

I took several long deep breaths before opening the door.

What the? Why do I have to question why someone is there when I open the door? Last time it was my best friend's ex. This time it's the person Riya stood up for on the day we went to the movies.

Did Riya give our address to a stranger? We met her once!

"Hi," I said, but it came out like a question.

"Oh! I didn't know you lived here! What a coincidence! I'm Riley, remember me?"

What does she mean by didn't know? I was with my wife that day!

"I remember you," I said. "I'm sorry, but can I help you?"

"My boyfriend invited me over. I'm assuming he's your brother?"

Oh. That explains everything. Ash should open the door for his girlfriend, who looks much better than when we saw her.

I invited her and told her I'll call Ash down.

"Riley's here," I told him.

He paused what he was doing. "You know her name?"

Even if I hadn't met her before, how dumb is he to think she wouldn't introduce herself?

"Considering we're meeting for the second time. Yes."

"What do you mean?" He asked.

I sighed. "You don't keep someone waiting."

"Right," he said and walked past me downstairs.

He's wearing my cologne! That's my most expensive cologne! Who let him into my things? And why did Riya let him pick the most expensive one? I thought having a sibling was hard, but having a wife who loves her brother-in-law is much more difficult.

He brought her back upstairs and is that my shirt? Really? He had full access to my closet.

"Keep the door open," I warned him before leaving.

I grabbed my phone, dialing my wife's number as I lay on the bed.

"Hey," she greeted. "Vihaan, say hi to my husband."

She's with my best friend? I've come to the conclusion Riya hates me.

"Hello, asshole!" Vihaan laughed.

"Right back at you," I said to him.

I asked Riya if she gave Ash access to my things.

"Ya. What're you going to do about it?" She challenged. "He said he invited his date home."

What am I going to do? What a lovely question.

"He's wearing my favorite shirt!" I whined.

"He's your brother! Relax."

Fine! I'll relax and let it be. If Ash ruins that shirt, I'm forcing him to buy a new one.

"What're you doing with Vihaan?" I asked.

"He's my friend. I told you I'm meeting a friend. Listen!"

I heard Vihaan laugh in the background. "He's jealous, Riya."

I am jealous! I won't even hide it.

Her voice indicated she was turned away from the phone. "He's been with you since kindergarten! I've known you for three years."

In my defense, she's known me for three years too!

She turned her attention back to me. "Actually, I'm holding your best friend at gunpoint to make a delicious meal I'm bringing home for Ash and his date. Whoever she is."

"You're in for a surprise," I told her. "You won't believe who it is!"

"You saw her? Is she pretty?"

That's a trick question. "Uummm sure. I can see she looks happier than when we lost her."

"We? Saw her?" She questioned.

She's trying to get me to give in. "No, princess. You have to come home and see for yourself. Wouldn't want to ruin the surprise."

"You're playing a game. Aren't you? To get me to come back. I'm staying with Vihaan then!"

I laughed. "I know where he lives and works."

"Was that meant to be a threat?" Vihaan asked. "Because it was a weak one. I know where you live and work, too, genius."

Where's Anaya when you need her?

"It's not a game nor a threat. I miss my wife!"

"You saw me an hour ago," Riya said.

"So? I can't miss you?"

She sighed. "Vihaan's almost done. I'll be home soon."

Yippee! "I'll see you then."

"Sounds good. Don't tell them to keep their door open so you can eavesdrop if he brings her upstairs. I trust Ash. I know he wouldn't even harm a fly."

"I know that," I said, trying to figure out how she figured that out. "And princess, I love you."

"I love you too. Sometimes."

I heard Vihaan burst out laughing in the back. I hadn't heard him laugh that loud since he hit me with a snowball back in third grade when I wasn't looking.

Riya had disconnected the call, so now I wait. Should I offer the kids something to eat or drink? Or is that the boyfriend's responsibility? Would I impose on the date if I did? See, I never dated so I don't know. I mean, technically, Riley is a guest. I could offer something.

I spent the longest time not only thinking but researching the question I had. Can't believe I have to Google if I can offer my brother's date a snack. This is what not dating does, apparently.

I wonder if our parents knew he was dating. I quickly created a group chat and asked them. They both replied with yes and dad even gave me the name.

Why was I the last one to know? That's unfair!

I heard the front door open and ran out of the room, past Ash's, to greet my wife. Riley is probably questioning my actions, while Ash is used to it.

"Hi princess," I said, kissing her.

"Hello. The kids upstairs?" She asked.

"Yes. Do you want me to get you anything?"

She shook her head. "I drank with Vihaan."

I stopped in my tracks. "You did what?"

"Drank with your bestie," she shrugged.

But drinking was my thing with Vihaan. They drink together? And I'm finding that out today? Next thing you know, Vihaan has already proposed and I'm unaware. I'll kill him if he doesn't tell me! I'm trying to plan the best bachelor party! I'll have newscasters there to capture it for the books.

"Riley!" Riya said, surprised when she saw.

Well, at least Ash left his door open.

"Hi Riya!"

Ash looked at both girls. "You two know each other?"

Riley answered. "She saved me from Jasper."

My brother's eyes went ice cold when she mentioned another man. Well, someone is about to be highly protective of his girlfriend.

Riley had gotten up to hug Riya.

"I didn't know you both were around the same age," Riya was still surprised.

He looked over at me, still mad, it seemed. "What did you do with her ex? Please tell me you tortured him. Maybe how you did it..."

Riya quickly avoided remembering that situation. "I have food! It's from this Michelin star chef that my husband is friends with."

Riley looked at the bag. "I bet it's delicious! I'm starving."

I looked over at Ash. I gave him a look that said, "D*ude, why didn't you offer her anything?"*

He didn't respond to that. He still seemed angry. Alright, note to self, keep an eye on this man before he ends up in prison. Jasper is already in jail, but my brother will kill him if that guy gets bailed out.

"So, how did you two start dating?" I asked.

"He saved me from getting killed. I was at my dad's house for something. Thankfully, I left the door open. Dad began yelling at me, I think it was about gambling me off and he was passing by on his bike. Heard the yelling and shattering of glass and just ran into a stranger's house to save me."

If Riley and Ash worked out, both of our wives would be coming from traumatic pasts.

Ash said, "I had no idea it was even her in that house. After everything Anaya and Riya went through, I learned so much more about abuse. I told myself I'll help anyone whenever I can. Didn't know I'd end up saving the person I was crushing on."

I love how both of them blushed.

Riley added. "Funny enough, I had a crush on him too. I didn't tell him anything while he got me checked into the hospital or while we were there. Kissed him on the walk home because who would walk seven miles with someone from their class back home? They'd put me into a taxi and say we wish you the best. He kissed me back like I was made for him. I wanted to take him home right then and there."

I stopped her. "Woah! TMI! Don't need to hear what you did with my brother afterward!"

She laughed. "I meant take him home because I felt safe for the first time in someone's embrace. I just didn't want to be alone. We haven't done anything. He understands the trauma I went through. I love him so much for that."

"I love you too," Ash said, kissing her cheek.

"Kids, no PDA. Varun doesn't seem to like it," Riya smiled.

"Kids?" They both questioned.

I ignored Riya's comment. "Ash is younger than me so I've referred to him as the kid, child, or something similar whenever I was upset with him."

"Ah, I see."

Riya switched the topic to something much lighter. She never wants to talk about abuse and I don't blame her. She's been through a lot. Riya was telling Riley about Vihaan's restaurant, him being my best friend, the food and Anaya when Ash's phone went off with a text. He said it was Vihaan, ironically enough.

Why didn't he text me? I pulled my phone out to check, but nothing.

My brother's smile completely disappeared.

"What's wrong?" We asked.

Please tell me my best friend is okay. I got my phone ready to text Anaya in case anything did happen.

"Anaya," he barely spoke loud enough, as if he was in disbelief. "She broke up with him."

This has to be a joke. I closed my texting app. This is a joke. Anaya wouldn't hurt him like that. I left the room, grabbed my keys and sped. Anaya wouldn't hurt him. Would she?

Chapter 14

The guy in the brown jacket has been following me around. Could he be associated with the anonymous text messages?

"I'm sorry to ask," I told the cashier. "Could someone walk me to the car? I'm being followed."

I pointed out the man, around 5'5, skin as pale as winter and now pretending to look at something else.

"Definitely," he replied. "It's nothing to apologize for. Better safe than sorry. I'll get someone for you right now."

I went to guest services, pretending I had to make a payment while waiting. A male worker, around 6'3, introduced himself to me and helped me walk to my car. At the same time, another person distracted the man following me.

I thanked the worker before he left. I locked my doors and drove away as fast as I could. I usually don't even start driving without music, but this wasn't the time to decide what I wanted to listen to.

I'll have to tell Varun about this. In case it happens again, I want him to be aware. I've still not told him about the text messages and I don't plan to. I'm worried he'll monitor my phone.

As if this shock wasn't enough, my display showed Anaya was calling. Why is she calling me?

"Hello," I said. I'm still upset that she left Vihaan to go back to Oregon. Her excuse isn't something I'm falling for. She's hiding something from all of us.

"Hi. Are you busy?" She asked.

"That depends on what you want to talk about," I stated.

"Riya, I know you don't want to talk to me after what I did and that's fine. I called to ask you how he's holding up."

She's joking right now. If she cares so much, why didn't she call him? Why did she break up with him?

I merged onto the freeway. "Like you care."

I must have hit her on the heart since the line remained silent.

"Riya," she finally said, but I didn't let her continue.

"He tried to drink his way to death, Anaya! Varun had to hide all the alcohol at our house and the restaurant. Only Vihaan's employees know where it is. You are so stupid! You have no idea how much he loves- no, let me correct that. You have no idea how much he loved you."

I had to use past tense. Vihaan still loves her, but she doesn't deserve to know that.

I added, "Don't try to contact him anytime soon. He's not himself right now and anything could upset him. You need to get your shit together. Stop breaking his heart any chance you get!"

"What the fuck do you mean by any chance?" She asked.

Oh, she's mad? Does she have a right to be angry?

"You know what I mean. We thought we'd have to take him to the hospital for alcohol poisoning. You broke him!"

I pulled up to the driveway and went straight inside. I would have finished this conversation in the car had I not been followed earlier.

I put my things down. "Anaya, enjoy Oregon. Don't ever come back to New Jersey. Nobody wants to deal with you right now. We don't want to see you."

Varun walked in and heard me say that. He sat down while I changed the call to speaker mode and rested in his embrace. Have to be sure to tell him that I got followed around after this conversation ends.

"Wow," she scoffed. "Here I was thinking I had a friend."

"I was your friend until you hurt my brother-in-law. Now, I'm wondering if everything you ever said to him was real. Maybe you were still stuck on the fake dating aspect of things."

I didn't want to fight with her, but I also wanted her to come to her senses. How does she not know Vihaan and her are made for each other? How?

"Fake dating? You know what, Riya? At least I'm not with someone who cheated on me!" She hung up the call immediately after saying that.

I'm boiling with anger now! Varun had to hold me as he kept apologizing for what happened over three years ago. However, he's not the one who should be apologizing.

He stopped only when he looked towards the door. I turned my head to see Vihaan standing there.

Shit! How much did he hear?

"Vihaan," Varun said quickly, getting up and being by his side. "Come sit with us."

He shook his head. "Riya, I'm so sorry for what she said to you. You didn't deserve that."

"Vihaan, you don't have to apologize. I do something else maybe both of you should be aware of," I said to change the topic.

I told both men about being followed around in the store and how it wasn't the first time it had happened. It happened once before, but I was with Anaya, so I felt safe.

"Riya!" They both yelled at me.

Vihaan continued, "We're going to be watching you. You'll be dropped off and picked up."

Varun added, "I agree. You won't be going anywhere alone. Not anymore."

Both guys started arguing about my safety and I had no choice but to let them argue with me. At least, it's keeping Vihaan distracted.

Vihaan

Chapter 15

Pick up the damn phone! Come on, Anaya, this is our fight! Pick up the phone. Let's talk like adults.

"Hello," someone else answered.

"I need to speak to Anaya," I told her.

"She's busy. Who's this?" The voice, I now figured out, belonged to her cousin. I met her family when we flew to Oregon together.

"It's Vihaan."

"Oh! I'll get her right now," she said as I heard the phone be placed on what sounded like a table.

I waited three minutes until I finally heard Anaya say hello. I'm not going to let her voice affect me. I can do this.

"Why did you tell Riya what you do? That wasn't nice of you," I said, reminding myself I was doing this for Riya only. That was her best friend!

"She told you?" She asked, surprised.

"I heard everything. Anaya, I'm the person you hate. I'm the one you want nothing with anymore. I'm the one who you think wouldn't give up anything for you. I'm the one you need to take everything out on. Don't bring others into it. You have to apologize to her."

"Wow. I never thought the day would come when I'd see you mad. Funny, it's for another woman."

What the hell did Oregon do to her? That's not the Anaya I know.

"Anaya, what's going on? You're not the type of person to act up," I said, realizing she could be in trouble.

"Why do you care? I have to go."

"No! You don't have to go. Answer my question," I almost commanded her.

"I do have to go. We have different things to accomplish in life. I need to go," she added that last part as if she'd get caught speaking to me right before hanging up.

I told myself I'd block her number when I was done with this phone call, but I couldn't bring myself to. I need to know what's wrong with Anaya.

Riya

I was wrong if I thought only two men would be adamant about picking and dropping me off. There are four!

"Hi Ash," I said as I got in the car.

"Hi bhabi. How was work?" He asked as we drove off.

"Good. You have class in a bit. Why are you here?" I asked.

"Dad's going to take you from college. I had time to get you, so why not? Plus, your workplace is close to college."

Those were the other two, Ash and my father-in-law. If you think men can keep their mouths shut, you're wrong. Varun immediately told everyone and now I have four men almost rotating shifts. They even have a group chat where all they ask is who's dropping me off and picking me up. Most of the time, Varun drops me off, but with his schedule, he rarely gets to pick me up. Having rotating people helps because every week, the schedule changes, so if I was still being followed, it'd be hard to get leads.

Sure enough, dad was already waiting for me when we arrived. How did he not get a parking ticket for being here without a pass?

"Thank you," I said to Ash.

"Don't mention it. Gotta go to my boring lecture. See you at home," he waved.

Dad got out of the car and opened the door for me. Something all men do, I noticed. Regardless of the relationship, they always get out to check the area and open the door.

"Thank you," I said as we drove home.

"You don't have to thank me. We have this conversation weekly," my father-in-law said as he smiled.

My phone vibrated in my pocket as I reached to dig it out. I looked at the time and thought it was Varun, but it wasn't.

EX BESTIE- Riya, I was told to apologize to you by Vihaan so sorry. Happy?

EX BESTIE- you can show him this so he knows I did

What is her problem? Something in that text is screaming help me. What's going on with her? This isn't the Anaya I've known for the past three years. Maybe we should go to Oregon and figure it out. The question becomes, would she be at her house or somewhere else?

Chapter 16

Something seemed like it was going to go wrong today. I had this feeling in my gut that it would, but I wasn't sure what it could be. For safety purposes, I packed pepper spray and shared my location with Varun. Thankfully, I was born before technology took over, so I was used to memorizing phone numbers, in case anything did happen where I wouldn't have my phone.

"Good morning, Riya," my coworker Ari brightly greeted me. She was a morning person, but I was not. I didn't understand people who could be so bright at work. I had thought I wanted to work, but now that I did, I hated my job. Same shit, just a different day.

"Good morning, Ari. You are bright as usual," I said, trying not to sound dismissive.

"Always!" she cheered before going to her desk.

Seriously, it was nine o'clock on a Thursday morning. Even the weather was dark and cloudy, so I really didn't understand where she got the energy. Must be her recent divorce from an abusive husband because nothing else made sense to me.

At 9:30 am every Thursday since I started, we had a team meeting. It was getting close to promotions, which, considering I had been working here for four years now and was one of the top employees, I was hoping I would get. If not, I was going to quit and work somewhere else. I didn't care how many times Varun told me that we had enough money where I didn't need to work, I was going to get out of the house and work. No way was I going to relive the past I had.

"I have never seen you nervous," I told Ari as we entered the meeting room. She was the one presenting for our team today. "Just bright and happy."

"I'm just hoping I did enough before I get yelled at by our grumpy boss again."

Grumpy was an understatement for our boss. At fifty-two and single, he took all of life's frustrations out on us, especially us married women. How was it our fault nobody ever dated him? Maybe if he wasn't such a grade A asshole, someone would have thought about it. He tried to withhold promotions for women, and even the men that worked here were against that, since they saw how hard some of us worked. I was lucky I had interviewed and gotten an offer for another place called Kaur's Kolkwitzia. I did have my cousin help me out there, though, since her place wasn't hiring at the moment. She did say I could work for her as soon as there was an opening until I would work at Kaur's Kolkwitzia; it just depended on if I got the promotion.

Varun was iffy about moving to the West Coast when I told him about the job interview and how I got the role. He had grown up on the East Coast, and it was his home. He wasn't too sure he wanted to leave everything he knew, but he came around to it because, in the end, as long as we were together, he didn't care where we were. Also, he still had to do everything I said, considering what he had done with Camren the day of our *roka.*

"You got this! Woman up!" I told her as our boss walked in.

He scoffed at the part where I said, "Woman up," and I was this close to going off on him.

"Ready?" he asked Ari as everyone got settled.

She nodded. I had never seen this girl anything but bright. However, here she was nervous, stuttering, and just an overall wreck.

Our boss told her in front of everyone, "Maybe if you manned up instead, you could have done better."

I spoke up before anyone else could, "Maybe if she did, she would be as single as you are. At least she has a spouse."

Nobody in our office except for Ari and I knew that she was in an abusive marriage or that she was divorced. She wanted to keep it that way, and I respected her privacy and her wishes.

I ignored the looks I was getting from the rest of the team when I added, "It must suck that nobody ever even had a crush on you. Fifty-plus years of never being liked would do that to you—you know, become an arrogant, good-for-nothing, sexist, racist son of a bitch."

"Watch your mouth, young lady!" he yelled at me.

"Why? I am no longer working for you! I don't need to wait until I get a promotion because you know what, I don't need to be bitched at again." I had already gotten a lot of that growing up. "I quit!"

I enjoyed yelling that in his face as I slammed the door behind me, went to my desk, and gathered my things. I couldn't wait to tell Varun what had happened, knowing he would be so proud that I stood up not only for Ari but also for myself.

Ari came to my desk as I was gathering my things, and I smiled at her. She said, "I just wanted to let you know that I was thankful for what you did there. I actually quit as well because I got a better role closer to home. No more commuting!"

"That's great! I am really happy to hear that, and you don't have to thank me. I want to see how his company survives when he loses the top two performing employees."

"It'll tank for sure. I really do hope we can keep in touch though," she said.

"Of course. Message me whenever, and I will fly back to the East Coast." I hugged her goodbye and went to my car.

I decided to make a little stop to get a cake. The decorator looked at me confused when I asked if she could write "I quit" on it. She probably was used to writing "Happy birthday" or "Happy anniversary." The only thing bothering me was the area in which this shop was located, and I left my spray in the car. I thanked the shop owner before going about my day.

I knew something bad was going to happen today because as soon as I stepped outside and walked towards my car, I was blindfolded and couldn't breathe.

All I could remember was being dragged and thrown inside the trunk of a car when I regained consciousness.

Who the fuck kidnapped me? I am going to kill them! Where the fuck is my phone? In my car! I left the fucking phone in my car.

Where was the glow-in-the-dark pull tab on this car? I did remember some law saying all cars needed to have one if they were made after 2001, so I just needed to find it, pull it, and kick my way out, but no luck. This person probably prepared their car before.

Fuck!

All I could do now was kick out the lights or punch them out. This asshole was in such a hurry he didn't even tie me down, so it worked better for me. It took several tries before I finally did it, but that was when the vehicle came to a stop.

Shit! I am dying here!

I tried my best to take a peek. I could see through the broken light and started to wave like crazy to alarm people someone was in the trunk. My kidnapper had walked away without realizing what I had done.

"Are you okay? The cops will be coming soon," I heard a male voice say.

I knew that voice. I vaguely remembered hearing it. If I could see his face, I would know, but that voice was too familiar. Another familiar voice joined him, another male. I needed to know who these people were. I could barely make out their faces right now.

Once the cops arrived—thankfully quickly—and I was let out, they asked me several questions, of which I knew the answers to only a few. Then they went inside to find the criminal. Seriously, why not just wait here for when he comes back to his car?

I turned back to see who the guy was since the other had left along with the police.

"Ryan!" I said, surprised.

"Riya! What the hell are you doing getting kidnapped?" he asked. Still the same, on-edge, worrisome, Ryan that I had known.

"Oh, you know, just checking to see if kicking the lights out would work," I sarcastically told him.

"Hilarious."

"I wasn't planning on getting kidnapped, Ryan. You are going to tell my cousin, aren't you?"

"Without a doubt. I literally live in their house! Mia is going to go insane when she finds out," he told me.

I had known that Ryan and his brother weren't Mia's real family, but she sure as hell treated them like they were. Mia had gotten married prior to my elopement. I remembered my husband going insane since it had been a destination wedding that I had attended with my parents. He had been blowing up my phone, worried about my safety.

"Then we just don't tell her," I suggested. That was a bad idea because Ryan told everyone everything.

His brother, Abhi, had gone to the school Ryan worked in and forced him to sign a contract that not only gave up 50 percent of what Abhi had owned but also forced Ryan out of the place he had to live in the mansion-like place Abhi owned. I had been to California once to visit Mia, but that was way before I found out Abhi wasn't actually Mia's real brother.

"Nice try, Riya. Let your husband know that you are going back with us," he said as Abhi joined us.

"Riya! What the hell? How the hell did you get kidnapped? My sister is going to flip out! She will fly over here the minute she finds out!" Abhi said, also freaking out.

I really liked that Abhi still referred to Mia as his sister after knowing the truth.

"I repeat two things: one, we don't tell her, and two, I wasn't planning on getting kidnapped! What the hell are you both doing on the East Coast anyways?"

"Business trip," they replied.

Ryan added, "Apparently saving your ass too."

"You're lucky I like you, Ryan, otherwise I wouldn't be appreciating that tone right now," I told him.

I let them know I didn't have my phone, so Abhi let me use his. Thank God, I was born before 2000, when writing down and remembering numbers was a thing.

"What the fuck do you mean 'funny story'? How is that a funny story? And you are going with two other men now?" Varun questioned after I told him everything. He was understandably very upset and would not rest until I was back safe with him.

"Technically, if Mia is my cousin, that makes Abhi my adopted cousin, and Ryan is his brother," I calmly let him know.

"Vihaan and I are coming to pick you up. Stay safe until then because I swear to God, I will kill them if they lay a finger on you," he said and hung up.

"I look forward to meeting your husband. He sounds lovely," Ryan sarcastically said, laughing.

"Drop the attitude, or I'll tell Nancy you let a woman into your hotel room," I replied, giving Abhi his phone back.

"You definitely are related to Mia," Abhi said. "Let's get you somewhere safe. I believe the cops have custody of him now."

I nodded, and we left.

Varun

Chapter 17

I dragged Vihaan out of his house to go to this hotel with me. After his and Anaya's breakup, he took it really hard on himself to the point where he would just go to work and then come home. I never thought these two would break up years into the relationship. I was always waiting for him to tell me that he proposed, so when the evening he told me they broke up, I laughed, thinking it was a prank that he and Ash were pulling on me. He didn't tell me for a bit, just kept taking shots until I had to take the alcohol away. When he did tell me the reason they broke up, I thought it was one of the most ridiculous reasons I had ever heard.

"Wait." I put my drink down. "You serious? You actually broke up?"

Vihaan nodded as he took another shot.

"What happened?"

No answer.

"Something had to have happened. I can't help you out if I don't know it."

He still didn't answer and just poured himself another shot.

"Vihaan! Quit drinking and answer me."

No luck. I took the alcohol away and waited for him to answer the question. I didn't mean to be a pushy friend, but I just needed to know so I could help him out.

"She said that we both have different goals in life and we should go our separate ways," he finally answered.

'That's ridiculous,' I thought. 'There has to be another reason because I know Anaya, and I know that is not a reason she would break up with him. Maybe he just took too long to propose or something, but there is no way that is a reason for these two to break up, knowing how much they love each other. Something worse had to be happening behind the scenes to her. These two love each other more than they love anyone or anything.'

"You just let it happen?" I asked, still trying to figure something out.

"I want her happy," he sighed. "Happiness hurts. Can you give me the alcohol back, please?"

"No, I am not going to let you drink your way to death. There has to be something she didn't tell you."

I asked Riya if she could come out to the backyard. Riya and Anaya shared almost everything with each other. Just as Vihaan and I were best friends, our partners had become besties as well. She had to know something or have a hint as to why they broke up.

"What do you mean they broke up? That's not even possible! I won't be fooled just because it's April first today," were the first words Riya said when I told her.

I suggested she just take a look at the amount of alcohol Vihaan had consumed, and that made her believe me.

"I'm sorry, but I actually don't know anything about this. Anaya never told me that they broke up. I am just finding out right now. I will call her later. She probably thought I would tell you, so maybe that is why she didn't tell me," she suggested.

That did sound like something that was possible.

"Can I crash here tonight? I don't think I am going to be able to drive back," Vihaan said, taking another shot.

'How did he even get the drinks back?'

I had put them away and out of his reach. He had to have taken them when I took Riya to the side to talk with her. Having the conversation in front of my friend was a bad idea, but apparently, leaving him alone was worse.

"You can sleep here. I am going to make a phone call," Riya said and left.

I took the drinks away from Vihaan again and told him to get ready for bed instead. He really did have more than he could handle because he was already wobbly when he stood up. This was going to be a long night and an even longer morning. He chose the right day to show up, since his restaurant was closed tomorrow. I helped him get to the guest room and told him to just message me if he needed anything. He didn't even take his breakup with Camren as bad as he took this one.

I went to my room and changed before Riya walked in, looking defeated.

"Nothing good came out of the call?" I asked.

"It's ridiculous. Apparently, they want different things in life and have different goals. I know it's not my place or our place to say this, but I know he would have given up everything he had to help her out. She's moving back to the west coast. I am going to fly to Oregon and kick her ass because that is one of the stupidest reasons I've ever heard. She is not going to be happy with anyone else. Mark my words, I will kick her ass. She may be the only friend I have, but she's going to get it."

"Come here, princess. It's not our fight to fight," I told her.

"But both our friends are going to get hurt. Look at Vihaan—he's already a mess, and I know Anaya will be one too. She probably already is. She may think she can move on, but I can guarantee you that no man is going to treat her the way Vihaan did. Nobody will love her the way he did."

"We can help them out, but we can't make the decision for them."

"I am going to look at flights. You should sleep, since you have work tomorrow."

"I will, but I am going to be worried about him all day at work."

She smiled. "Finally worrying about someone that isn't me. I am off from work tomorrow, since my boss and some people have a conference to go to. I will look after him, and your parents are home as well."

"I always worry about you. Vihaan didn't even take his break-up with Camren as bad as he took this one. I hid all the alcohol before he could start thinking his breakfast, lunch, and dinner are drinks. If he asks where the booze is, tell him you don't know anything about it. If you want to make him breakfast, two eggs with some avocado toast will help, since his ass was drinking so much. Don't feel that you have to make that, though. I know that you had to cook for everyone in the past, so it's your choice."

"I'll do it. Don't stress yourself out and get some sleep. I will take a page out of your book and text you updates, hourly."

"See, you did learn something from me. Goodnight, princess."

We arrived at the hotel where Riya had texted us. I was pretty sure this was Vihaan's first time seeing the sun or even the outdoors in a while. He still didn't say much on the drive to the hotel, but he was speechless when I told him why I was dragging him along.

I knocked on the door. A man, who was about 5'7", dressed like a CEO, and had eyes that gave away the fact he should have been getting more sleep, opened it.

"Can I help you?" He politely asked.

I responded with the same politeness, "I'm here for Riya. I am her husband."

All of his politeness disappeared. "How do I know you are her husband and not her kidnapper's assistant?"

"Why don't you ask her?" I retorted, and he turned around to do so.

Who the hell was this man? How dare he question the relationship I had with my wife? How do I know he wasn't involved in the kidnapping? I could have brought the cops with me. What if they made her lie and say that she knew them?

He opened the door to let us in. I hugged Riya right away and kept asking if she was fine. I didn't let her go at all when the same guy had asked if I had any leads on who could have done this. The only people I could think about were her immediate family, but they were deported back to their home country almost three years ago.

"I will have my people look into it," the other man said. This one had light brown round eyes, dark black, short, curly hair, and brown skin. His face was oval-shaped, and his voice was so soft. "I'm Ryan, by the way, and that's my brother, Abhi. Don't mind him, he's a bit hot-headed."

I shook his hand, and Vihaan did as well, introducing himself.

"You have people that can look into this kind of stuff? Are you associated with the FBI?" I asked, and that got his brother to laugh out loud.

"See, everyone thinks you are associated with the FBI," his brother said, laughing so much he could barely get the words out.

Ryan shook his head. "I just happen to know people. Feel free to give me a call if you get any information or have an idea of who it could be. Here's my information."

I took the card while he turned to his brother to say, "At least I am on a talking basis with my wife and not back in the enemies stage."

That got his brother to be quiet real quick.

"She did that to herself," Abhi stated before turning his attention back to us. "Feel free to let us know if you are ever in California. It's better if you stay with us than having Riya in some hotel or Airbnb where she could be targeted. We have good security, actually one of the best in the system. Someone is always home, so she won't be alone. Plus, Riya is Mia's cousin, which makes her my cousin, even if I was adopted."

'Right! Riya did mention her cousin. I wonder if she told them about her job and moving to the west coast. From the looks of it, she hasn't yet because he did say, "if you ever are" and not "when you are" in California.'

"I will have the same security cameras shipped over to your place by the end of the day," Ryan added. "Mia would be very disappointed if I did nothing to help prevent something like this from happening again."

He also told Vihaan that he would send some for his restaurant as well, since whomever did this could have possibly known that Riya and I love to go to his place to eat. I was assuming Riya had mentioned that earlier to them while it was just the three of them.

"Are you in the Mafia?" I asked.

How did he have people that get something so fast out here if he was from the west coast?

"The what? No! I used to work as a high school counselor before this one," he pointed to his brother, "forced me to sign the contract. He showed up with it at my job, told me to sign it, and now we work together at the business our dad used to own before he passed away."

"Oh, I am sorry for your loss," Vihaan said.

"It's okay. We were both very young when our parents passed away."

"Both of them?" Vihaan asked.

Abhi answered, "Dad passed away, and Mom was murdered. I had no idea we were brothers, since we got adopted into separate families, until he told me. Couldn't stand him in college, and he didn't tell me until years after that."

"I'm so sorry to hear that," I said.

I couldn't even imagine losing both of my parents at a young age and then not seeing my little brother for that long. I would be bothering my adoptive parents to help me find my little brother.

"Enough of our sob story," Ryan said. "You all should head back, and we should leave as well. Our flight is in two hours, and the airport is a ways out."

We thanked them again before heading out. I made a mental note to ask Riya about getting a tracking device on her watch. She didn't have her phone with her, but she still had her watch, so it could help keep her safe. I made another note to look into her family's whereabouts because I just couldn't understand who else would do this.

Chapter 18

There's no more lotion. I should place it back and pretend that I never saw it. I know I'm safe, but the traumatized version of myself is still scared that anyone could change at any second.

I quickly put it back when I heard footsteps and ran to grab my laptop. I pretended I was looking something up when Varun walked in.

"Hi, princess," he greeted. "Sorry, I'm late. Got stuck in traffic. How was your day?"

He placed a kiss on my forehead. I'm not allowed to leave the house without anyone. I know it's for my safety, but it feels like being back to where I was. I don't know how to bring that up.

"Eh, the same. Did you eat something? I tell you to keep a snack for that reason."

"I did. What're you looking up?" He asked curiously as his eyes fell on the screen while he grabbed his water bottle.

Shit! The page had ads that were creepy and disturbing. Some about buying spiders from a man and calling him. Another is about selling some illegal stuff.

"I was just trying to look up a song stuck in my head," I lied. "Didn't know this would happen."

Varun grabbed the lotion bottle and I was quick to avoid any eye contact. Thankfully it was still winter, so I had my hands, which were now sweating, under the blanket.

He looked at the bottle and then opened the cap. I did that too. There was literally zero left. We both know it's even more important to keep our skin moisturized in the winter. Just as it's important to put sunscreen on throughout the year.

"It's empty," he said and looked at me.

Fuck!

"You want to go shopping?" He asked.

Wait a second. I was expecting something else.

"You? Want to go shopping?" I asked, dumbfounded.

He nodded. "I hate shopping, but I love spending time with you. Therefore, shopping with you, I don't mind that."

I let out a fake laugh that didn't sound fake.

"I'd rather stay in the blanket," I replied. "But I did find out that it was empty and didn't tell you. I didn't want you to be mad at me or blame me for finishing it like..."

"Like your family did," he finished the sentence for me.

Varun put the bottle back and sat by me.

"We've been married for how long now?" He asked as if he was doing an investigation.

"Four years as of yesterday," I answered.

"And how many times have I raised my voice or blamed you for anything in those three years?"

"Never. I knew you wouldn't, but I'm still traumatized by my past. All the abuse I suffered. It scares me that someday I might wake up to someone like them. They might decide that they want nothing to do with me. It terrifies me."

He didn't say anything. That's what I hated. I hated when he didn't say a word. I wish I knew what he was thinking.

"Riya, nobody here is going to hate you ever. Regardless of what you say or do."

I didn't say anything to his statement. Instead, I said, "Wounds that don't heal risk bleeding on those that never hurt you."

He got up and by my default, being abused, I thought I pissed him off. I probably did because he left the room. I should learn to shut up. My parents were right. I do talk too much.

Varun came back about ten minutes later with a snack for me. I was expecting something different.

"You need to eat something so we can go out. I'm not going to work tomorrow, so we'll stay out as late as you'd like. And yes," he faked a sigh. "We can go to Target."

I stopped chewing on the apple he had cut up for me. "Unlimited budget?"

"I might regret this, but when is my budget not unlimited for my wife?"

I threw the blanket off and ran to the closet he had built. I wasn't kidding when I said he'd be the one to fill it up with everything for me. I even had an unnecessary amount of PJs.

I wore a pair of jeans, boots, a black turtleneck and a black Trench coat. I added a pair of small silver hoops and the necklace he'd bought me on our first birthday. Didn't care about makeup right now.

"I'm ready!" I told him as we both looked at the time.

"It took you five minutes to get ready because I suggested going to Target?" He questioned, still looking at the clock.

"No. It took me six minutes to get ready because my husband had given me an unlimited budget. I always find unnecessary items there. What's the next Holiday?"

“Valentine’s day,” he said as if I asked the most ridiculous question.

“Ew, pass. We can get ready for the super bowl instead! Have a whole watch party!”

“I don’t even watch football!”

“I do,” I stated. My brother-in-law got me into it. “And so does your money, so let’s go.”

I took his hand and dragged him out while he was saying, “I really regret ever setting an unlimited budget for you.”

Varun

Chapter 19

We arrived in California a few weeks ago and I told Vihaan to fly his ass out here. He was still moping around on the east coast. I asked Abhi if that was fine and he had no problem with it. Abhi seems like a jerk from the outside but he is a really kind person on the inside.

The place he owned was a mansion with so many bedrooms, a theater, two offices, a nice backyard and a room that he kept locked. I asked him out of curiosity what that room was because if I was staying here until we got our own place I didn't need it creeping me out every time I walked past it.

"It's the library. I built it with Ishan and Ryan for my wife a few years ago and she started hibernating in it. I didn't care for that but I warned if she ever burned herself again I would dismantle it. I didn't have the energy or the time, as you can see I am all over the place, so I just locked it. I would have unlocked it the first time she apologized but then she said fictional men are better than me, so we keep it 'locked' now," he laughed. "It paid off because her business skyrocketed after that, since she put more attention towards that. She has people flying in from all over the world to work with her, not just the country. Instead of thanking me, she keeps telling me to unlock it."

"You built a library for your wife?" Riya asked joining us.

"Hey! I do things for you too!" I protested.

Abhi shook his head smiling. "Neeti loves to read. She always found comfort in books that she didn't have growing up. Coming from a family that had mentally and emotionally abused, gaslighted her, and more, she found books to be her escape from the reality she lived in. It took her years to build her trust in me because I was her reality, plus we didn't get along since high school. The two of us caused a lot of chaos, but that is a whole book on its own. The funny thing is I used locked in quotes because I unlocked it forever ago, she just never has the time to check it so I play along. She thinks we hit our enemies stage again, when in reality, I am just having some fun. I love her too much to ever hurt her. We both had different goals in our lives and we worked alongside each other to help the other out. Relationships are all supporting each other, especially when in a marriage. If she had a busy day, I would wake up and prepare breakfast and lunch for her. If I have a busy day she would yell at me to go to bed by eight so I could be well rested. She would have breakfast and lunch packed for me as well. That was before Ryan's in-laws moved in with us, now they do all the cooking and we work still supporting each other. It's why we turned one of the downstairs rooms on the side to an office, so Neeti's clients can enter through the door and not come into the house."

"I'm home!" Someone said getting our attention.

"This idiot is Ishan. He's my best friend and my biggest headache, who doesn't live here," Abhi said. "That is his wife Ellie and this little munchkin that glues herself to me is named Samiya."

"Hello, welcome to California," Ishan said cheerfully as I introduced myself and Riya.

"Abhi, did you unlock the library yet or is that the first thing I am going to have to hear again when I go see my bestie?" Ellie asked him as he played with the kid.

"Tell your bestie it's not locked,"he replied.

She sighed, "I hate coming here."

Ellie asked Riya if she would like to join them so that just left us guys and their daughter. Ellie wasn't even Indian but both Abhi and Ishan spoke to her in Punjabi. I may not be Punjabi but I can speak the language and understand it. I think it's cute they want Samiya to learn both languages because Ellie spoke to her Spanish before leaving. She is going to be bi-lingual before she even starts kindergarten, which I brought up in conversation with Ishan. He was such a bubbly person, I felt I had known him since birth.

"Nancy also teaches her some Vietnamese and Italian. She is a very spoiled kid because she is the only kid and she knows that if she asks her uncle for anything she will get it. That's a habit we have been trying to get her to quit. Plus, she takes advantage of the fact that he is both her *Chacha* - dad's brother and Masar - mom's sister's husband, so she gets a two in one. She calls him chacha and Neeti *massi - mom's sister* instead of *chachi*- dad's brother's wife. It's kind of funny. She's going to turn four in four months, time flies man."

"Let me spoil her in peace!" Abhi warned him. "I have enough money to do so. She isn't the only kid in the family. I still have Lily and Manish."

"Save it for when Neeti kicks you off the balcony for not unlocking her library. How are they doing anyways?"

"I repeat, it is not locked. They are good bro, Jessi is doing a great job raising them."

Abhi was telling me who Lily and Manish were as Vihaan joined us introducing himself to Ishan. I didn't even ask him about who they were, he just let everything about them spill.

"I know you! You are a michelin-star chef! Veg Spice Cafe!" Ishan was buzzing with excitement. "Are you staying here or just visiting because I would love to have a meal prepared by you. Don't worry I will have Abhi pay for us."

Same friendship Vihaan and I have displayed right there.

"No daddy pay! Chachu no pay!" Samiya protested and Ishan looked disappointed at her, while Abhi laughed.

"That's right. You tell him that my money is for you," Abhi told her.

"Seriously? Whose child are you?"

Vihaan told him there was no need to pay him, he would love to cook for us.

"Holy shit! You are Vihaan Armani! Abhi, why is there a Michelin star chef at your house? Not that mind, he's really good looking. You're single?"

"Mia, please stop it! For the love of God you are married! We had a whole destination wedding for you. Quit embarrassing me every chance you get. What are you doing here anyways?"

"I live here you asshole! How many times do we have to go over this?" Mia asked as she greeted me with a hug. She was the cousin that had spoken to me on the phone while I went insane checking to see if Riya was safe every five minutes. She got Riya the job she had with Neeti and would be taking Riya under her wing in about a month since someone put their two week notice in.

I loved that Neeti worked the office she had here most of the time so Riya was technically working from home. It was something we all agreed on for her safety. If Neeti had to go out of the office for other work, Riya was to stay here. Neeti could kick someone's ass no doubt about it from all the stories I have heard, but nobody wanted to risk anything.

I excused myself to check on Riya while everyone else was talking but Ellie was already headed back. She took me to the side before anyone could see.

"Neeti had a client that came in and Riya recognized her. Do you maybe know anything about this because I haven't seen Riya lose her shit since the time she's been working here. Granted, it's been a little bit of time but Neeti had to interfere. Riya's on timeout at the moment because we don't yell at clients."

There's only one person that could make Riya lose her mind.

"Where is Riya?" I asked.

"She's outside with Nancy's mom. I was just curious if you knew anything because then I could let Neeti know. If this is going to be a problem then Neeti can go to the clinen't place instead of her coming here."

Riya was with someone so that's good. I will speak to her about it later but I first let Ellie know what had happened on the east coast and why she was acting this way towards Anaya.

"Thank you. I will let Neeti handle the situation as she sees fit. Come on, let's go join the others," she said. "Let Riya be with Nancy's mom for a bit. It's better that she is with her."

I nodded and joined the others again. I couldn't concentrate on any conversation happening around me knowing that Anaya and Vihaan were at the same place, at the same time and yet the goal was to get them to avoid each other. Riya and I knew that our goal was the complete opposite but for Neeti's business benefit we couldn't say anything.

Neeti was the reason we had come to California, why we were able to stay here instead of a hotel, so we couldn't just ruin that.

Vihaan was finally smiling and happy with the people around him. I couldn't risk him going back to the state he was in, maybe it was best if we made them avoid each other.

He had prepared lunch for everyone, as I got Riya and Nancy's mom to join us. I get to have his cooking all the time so the compliments going on around the table didn't surprise me. He had that star for a reason. Vihaan had offered to take a plate to Neeti's office but Ellie told him to leave it because she won't eat when she's working. Abhi didn't know what was happening but agreed to what Ellie had said.

Riya and I exchanged glances before going back to our food.

"You have to feed her if you go in while she's working," Abhi told Vihaan. "Unless you feel like feeding her, your best bet is to just wait until she's done. I would also appreciate it if you didn't feed my wife. The image of someone else spoon feeding her doesn't sit right with me."

Once everyone was done with their lunch some of them went back to the living room and some went to the theater room he had. Abhi and I stayed behind offering to do the dishes.

"Abhi, you said that Ishan is your best friend. How would you react if he broke up with Ellie over something stupid?"

"He did one time. I wanted to kick his ass, but I also gave him the time he needed. She didn't take it back right away. He had hurt her a lot by breaking up with her so it didn't surprise me. I sided with both of them. Now, look at them. They have a beautiful daughter together and have been happily married for almost six years. I wasn't expecting them to have a kid that fast but they seem happy and their daughter is a blessing to all of us. What did Vihaan do?"

"That's his story to tell but I just wanted to help. The difference is he wasn't the one that initiated the breakup."

"Give him the time he needs. Encourage him to do what makes him happy while he adjusts to being single," he said putting the last of the dishes away. "I'm assuming that would be the girl."

I followed his gaze to where Anaya was now seated outside in the yard with Neeti, smiling and laughing. I looked over at Vihaan who was frozen in his spot. *Fuck!*

"You don't have to answer that, Varun. That is the girl, look at the way he's looking at her. She just flew in from Oregon this morning. Nancy picked her up from the airport before going to work at her boba shop, since it was an early morning flight and we all Nancy is the only one who'd willingly get up that early. She's a very nice person."

He went to open the screen door and tell them to come inside and eat something.

Anaya also froze for a second before acting like nothing happened. She can't be serious right now! How can she act like nothing happened? Does she not know how much she hurt him? What is wrong with her? How do people break someone's heart and then pretend that they never did anything wrong?

"Congrats on your wedding Anaya. I'm sure my wife will make you the most beautiful outfits," Abhi said. "You are more than welcome to spend the week you are in California here."

Wedding? No! Hell no! I will personally sabotage this wedding myself. I won't even hire anyone to do any of the dirty work, just going to show up and ruin it all. Sort of how she ruined my best friend's life. Vihaan stormed off as soon as Abhi said that. I should probably go after him but I was paralyzed by the word wedding.

"Will you unlock my library if I do?" Neeti asked before Avaya was about to say something.

"Who said I didn't already unlock it?" Abhi asked as he placed a plate for both the women.

Seems this is all they were going to talk about so I rushed to check up on Vihaan.

"She's getting married. She is fucking marying someone else after everything we went through," he was furious as I walked in. "She could have told me that. I would have rather heard that. I am not what she wants anymore! It sure as hell would have hurt a whole lot less. I shouldn't have gave her another chance that day in the hospital."

I was tearing up seeing him like this. Riya told me after their day in New York that both us and them had a second chance love story, under distinctive differences.

"Vihaan," I barely was able to speak.

"I can't do anything. She is in the same place as me, breathing the same air, at the same time and I can't do shit about it. I can't hold her, I can't bring myself to talk to her. I can't do anything."

My best friend was broken in front of me and I had no idea what I could do. Abhi told me I need to give him time, I doubt that would help in this situation.

"I'm going back home. I can't be here for my own well-being," he said. "Can you drop me off? I will get a flight back home this evening or at night time."

"Of course. I will ask Ryan if I could take his car. I am not going to stop you because as my best friend your mental and physical health comes first to me. I will have Esha keep tabs on you. Who knew your breakup would have her out of the house and following you around everywhere?"

After everything that happened between the two of us, I know what it took to get his apology and trust back. I am not the type of person that would ever destroy a second chance that was given to me.

He mustered a grin.

Everyone was in the backyard when we walked out except Riya who was just coming back from using the bathroom. She looked at him and then the suitcase before Vihaan had told her what happened.

"I'm sorry *bhabi* but I think it's best if I head out now," he added.

"It's the first time you referred to me as your sister-in-law. I won't stop you Vihaan because there's no reason to. I want you to promise me that you will call me when you land and when you are back home in Jersey."

"I will," he said, hugging her.

Varun

Chapter 20

I was able to purchase a space that was available to start my practice in California. It was a good thing I had saved up because I had no idea when life was going to throw a curveball in my direction, and I didn't want to bother asking anyone for the money. I never wanted to be one of those people that blew their money and then looked for help because they didn't have any. My parents taught us the value of money as we grew up, which stuck with me. I wouldn't just recklessly spend it whenever I wanted to. We would be returning to New Jersey once it was deemed safe enough for Riya to go back.

The hardest thing was getting new patients, since a majority of people had already established care with another optometrist. Should have just went the extra mile and became an ophthalmologist. I had to do my research on how I could find people, which actually wasn't too hard if you worked with the majority of the insurance companies. Still didn't understand why eye care was an add-on to health benefits. Health care would cover your entire body, but you needed to add your eyes and teeth from somewhere else, if it wasn't already included in the package. It was one of the reasons why during the holiday season, I tried to offer free exams to those people that couldn't afford it. Not only was the exam free, but if they needed glasses or contacts, those were free as well. Worked well every year, and since most eye exams were yearly, those people would book an appointment in December before leaving to secure their spot for the upcoming year. That was until I had to move, which was a mess because I wanted to ensure they got their exams, so I booked myself solid before the move to the point where I didn't see any of my family or friends until the Sundays because I worked Saturdays to help them out. My assistants didn't mind simply because they were getting paid for being there.

"I was wondering if I could get lasik, since my left eye has astigmatism?" my patient had asked me as I finished her checkup.

"Yes. Astigmatism doesn't disqualify you from getting lasik," I answered. "As long as it's the right type and falls under the treatment limits."

"Does insurance cover it?"

"It's not a medical necessity, so it won't be. Same would go if you wanted to have your teeth whitened by a dentist. What I can tell you is that there are some discounts available, so your best bet is to do some research into this."

"Thank you, doctor. I will do that," she said before leaving.

That wraps up the last patient for the day. I'm just happy I have some patients that gave me a chance. Majority of them said the reasons being that their doctor was too expensive (even with insurance), their doctor had moved, the location, and the atmosphere. I try to keep people with good vibes around, since I learned my lesson the hard way about keeping people around who have negative goals in life.

I went to my office right as my phone buzzed with Riya's name.

"Hi, princess," I said.

"You need to come to the house now!" She had some traces of panic in her voice as she spoke.

"Riya, please tell me you are safe because I will kill someone if you aren't," I said, locking up and getting into my car.

"Just please, come."

"I am already on my way."

"OK. Drive safe because a speeding ticket is expensive."

"I can throw the money in the cop's face. I am sure you are very aware of that, but because you said so, I will do as I am told and drive safe," I told her before disconnecting the call.

I probably will still speed if I have to. As long as I can see where the cops are and slow down, I should be able to safely make it home without seeing the colors: red, white, and blue flashing behind me.

I got to the house we were staying at around half an hour later.

Thank you traffic.

The first thing that caught my eye before even going inside was the broken window.

I don't know if that was aimed at Riya, but she had to be shaken up by the experience. She's been on high alert about her surroundings since she got kidnapped, and so have all of us. She is meant to be with someone at all hours of the day.

As I got closer, I realized whoever broke the window was aiming for her because that was the room we were staying in. Who else even knew that besides the people that lived here? This had to be an inside job, but I wouldn't jump to conclusions without getting evidence first.

Riya was sitting in the living room with Neeti and Ellie when I went inside. She was pale as winter when I saw her. The last time I had ever seen her that pale was the day I found her covered in her own blood while laying on the ground, lifeless.

"What happened?" I asked everyone, but no one in particular.

"Riya said she wanted to take a nap, since today was a very busy day. I told her that it was fine. Since everyone was home, she wouldn't have to worry about anything anyways. About forty minutes later, we heard the window break. The guys ran to check what had happened, then she came out of the room and told them someone tried to break in," Neeti answered. "We were trying to get her to relax, but she just wanted to be with you. The guys left a while back. Abhi went to file a police report to make it look like what Ryan was about to do would be very legal."

I am suspecting Ryan so much. He has people that he won't tell us about, he can get items shipped to wherever he needs with a one phone call, and he is the only one that has access to the camera footage. I am going to gather all this evidence and show him in court to a judge so they can lock him up.

I was already holding Riya before Neeti started speaking. She seemed to have calmed down with the other woman, but I felt her calm down even more a few minutes after I started holding her.

"Who exactly are Ryan's people?" I asked when Nancy joined us.

She also had just come home from work. Apparently, anyone that lived or visited this place was being called over for safety purposes. This was so whomever had done this wouldn't be able to target someone else. I doubted they had another target, but it could have happened.

"When Ryan got adopted, his new parents were a judge and a sheriff. Nobody ever found out they weren't his birth parents, and he kept it that way because he realized it could come in handy someday, which it did on several occasions. They had a special unit of detectives and officers that were reserved for him once he came clean about his mom's murder while trying to get Abhi back. They found out Abhi was his real brother, but Abhi's adoptive parents refused, so Ryan didn't get his brother back until after college. Whenever Ryan needs anything tracked, he just gets those people on the case," Nancy answered.

Still suspecting him because how does someone just have a unit on reserve? Is that even a thing? She was probably a supreme court judge, if that was the case.

Another thing I picked up on was how quiet Ellie was, and Ishan still hadn't shown up. I thought everyone was supposed to be here. Where was he then?

I am adding him to the list of people I suspect. I really still have this gut feeling that this was an inside job.

"We'll leave you two alone for a bit so you can talk things over," Nancy added. "Plus, I have no idea what happened. I was just told to come home, and if I didn't, he'd file for a divorce. Rude, but now I can see why he was being so commanding on the phone."

Once the three of them went somewhere else, that's when Riya told me what else had happened that caused her to be as pale as she was.

"She wanted to take a nap too, so I suggested she could sleep with me-" Riya began, but tears formed in her eyes, causing her to stop for a bit. Then, she continued, "When the glass broke, she was playing right in the area it all landed on. She got scraps of glass in her body, and there was blood just everywhere. I ran out of the room to tell the guys, since I was so worried. I should have known better. It's all my fault there is a three-year-old in the hospital, covered in blood right now. I should have told her to play outside. I should have known I was a target the whole time. I have been apologizing to Ishan and Ellie non-stop. I even offered to pay the hospital bill, but they declined it. They aren't even mad at me because they said nobody knew this was going to happen. I'd probably feel better if they had yelled at me because I knew I was a target."

Now it makes sense why Ishan wasn't here and why Ellie had been so quiet. Their daughter loved Riya so much that she would spend as much time as she could with her. I remember just last week, we were laughing and saying Abhi is going to be replaced as the favorite. Ishan has been removed from the suspect list.

"They are right. Nobody knew this was going to happen, so you can't blame yourself. Their daughter is going to be completely fine, and the window will be replaced with bullet-proof glass if needed. If you still want to do something, we can pay the bill for them or pay them back for the cost of it. The others are looking into who could have done this already, so you don't have to worry about anything. They will catch the person. Didn't you hear Nancy say that Ryan's parents were a judge and a sheriff? He grew up hearing these kinds of stories, so I am sure he will make sure that person is punished."

Even though I still suspected him, I didn't want to say that. *There will be time for it, but not right now.*

"The guilt is eating me alive, though," she said as the doorbell went off.

Who the fuck could that be?

Everyone had a key or knew the code, so that had to be a setup. Neeti suggested I take Riya somewhere else while she went to get the door. I wanted to know who it was, so I left Riya with the other two women and came back downstairs.

It ended up being Ryan again.

I'm this close to losing my shit.

"You wouldn't happen to know anyone by the name, Kirin?" he asked me as he told Neeti to leave.

Oh no. That's not possible, though. I made sure they all were deported back, so why would he ask that right now?

"Unfortunately," I replied.

"Ya, well, unfortunately, I happen to know this asshole," Ryan said, and I finally looked over to where he was pointing. "This is Ayaan. He worked together with Kirin to cause the damage because he wanted to get back at you both for their being kicked out of the house."

Kirin was Riya's eldest and cleverest brother. How the hell did he find someone that used to live here?

This doesn't add up in my head because if he only wanted to get back at Abhi and his family, why the kidnapping and prior events?

"Start speaking, or I will have to force it out of you, and you don't want me forcing it," Ryan warned Ayaan.

I had never seen anyone look scared of Ryan before. That would have been a Kodak moment, if the situation had been under other circumstances.

"Kirian told me that his friends from the east coast that kept in-touch with him had said Riya and Varun left to go to California. I wasn't sure what that had to do with him telling me, but I decided to go along because I was curious. California is huge, so the chances of anything relating to this house would be very slim. He had one of his friends fly out here, and he suspected this area because it's where their cousin was. I had completely forgotten about them, since they hardly ever visited. I didn't go to Mia's wedding, so it had been almost over a decade since I ever saw that family. Putting some puzzle pieces together, Kirian told me it would be the best way to kill two birds with one stone. I figured that he was right. It would help me get back at them for kicking me out, so I agreed to it."

So Ryan is innocent? I suspected the wrong person this whole time? In my defense, I did have my reasons and never thought that it would be her eldest brother plotting all of this from another country. Ayaan is Mia's real brother, which made him Riya and Kirian's cousin.

"What problem did you have with Riya that you thought traumatizing her would be the answer?" I asked, trying to control the urge to not beat the shit out of this guy right here, right now. It seemed Ryan had taken some care of that, though, judging from the blood on this man's face.

"I didn't have a problem with Riya. I just wanted to get back at these guys," Ayaan answered.

"Everything started when we were on the east coast, still. How do I know you had nothing to do with that?"

"I didn't. I only found out when you came to the west coast. He had hired one of his friends to get rid of her when you both were there, still in New Jersey, saying it was her fault they had to face humiliation when they went back to India."

Of course, they had to face humiliation. They deserved that for everything they had to done Riya. Actually, they deserve way more than just humiliation—they should have been ten feet under by now.

"You are going to apologize and tell Riya the whole truth," Ryan said.

"No, I don't want him to see her. It makes it more risky if he knows what she looks like. I will tell her everything later," I told him, and he agreed to it.

Ayaan didn't even bother apologizing yet. All he did was give his reasons, but I was still waiting for an apology for this behavior or for him to apologize on behalf of her brother.

Ryan turned his attention back to Ayaan, "I believe it's best if you left and never showed your face around here again. If Abhi shows up while you are here, you are going to be messed up so bad, an ambulance won't be able to do anything. They might pronounce you dead on the spot, so you better disappear."

That worked like a charm because he was out of there faster than the speed of light.

I left to check on Riya. I didn't know when the right time to tell her what had happened would be because she was still a bit shaken up from the experience. I didn't want to add to any of it, so I just let her be for the time being. She was more worried about Samiya and the condition she would be in just waiting for them to come home.

Abhi came back a few minutes later. His brother had pulled him aside to give the 411 of what had taken place.

Damn! Just a few minutes earlier, and I would have known why Ayaan left that fast at the mention of Abhi's name. I still want to know, though. I could ask Neeti, since she was here in the room that I was in with Riya, but that means Riya would hear everything, so I have to wait.

Abhi

"What the fuck do you mean Ayaan was here?" I asked, unsure I correctly heard my brother.

"I just told you everything. Word for word. I gave you what Ayaan said. He wanted revenge for being kicked out.

He joined forces with his cousin because two birds, one stone. If you were listening, you would know."

"Ryan, I am this close to treating you how I did in college."

"You love me too much for that now. Plus, I would like to remind you what I did for you and why I was friends with your wife," he smirked.

Every fucking time. My brother has to remind me, every chance he gets, that he was friends with Neeti because I fell in love with her and had to act like we were enemies far into our marriage.

I fell in love with her our senior year of high school, but "we" didn't hit the "lovers" part after such a long time. Even when I confessed that I was never her enemy, she couldn't say, "I love you" for the longest time.

"Wait. If Ayaan was here, then was Annie here too? Where's my wife?" I asked.

He looked at me with a grin. "Have you met your wife? If Annie was here, there would be a line of ambulances parked outside for each body part of Annie's that Neeti would have broken."

True.

I found her ability to fight extremely attractive. To be honest, it was why I'd pick fights sometimes with her. I have yet to be thrown off the balcony, though (her favorite threat). I *did* get a bloody nose.

"I'm going to let her know I'm back. Where is she?"

Ryan set his drink down. "I think she's picking the lock of the library."

I inhaled to make sure I didn't yell at my brother and then exhaled. I went to the library, and sure enough, she was there.

"It's not locked," I said.

I was expecting her to pick a fight with me about unlocking it, not for her to run into my arms and hug me so tightly. I was sure she thought I'd disappear if she let go.

"I'm okay. I'm safe," I constantly repeated for reassurance until she let go.

"You aren't hurt, are you? I will kick his ass if you are."

I moved aside to go remove the lock and show her it had been unlocked.

"I know you would, so I would have admitted right away if I was. You do look really good when you're kicking ass. Why else do you think I annoyed you from senior year of high school until the day I confessed?"

"You picked fights because you thought I was attractive when fighting? You really do need a brain scan."

Instead of replying to that, I just walked inside and grabbed the books she had annotated. She hated when I did that. Her excuse was that it was personal, but what kind of husband would I have been if I couldn't have brought her favorite scenes to life? Then, she would have just said fictional men were better than me. I didn't do well with fictional competition. I didn't need that because I was the jealous type.

I ignored her telling me to stop while she tried to grab the book out of my hands. I was taller than her, so she was currently jumping up and down while I read.

"Why are so many books enemies-to-lovers? Why? There are various other tropes in the world," I said, turning the page. "I'm on chapter three now, and they're already in love? That's not enemies-to-lovers. That's annoying. That's what that is. You paid for this trope, not insta-love."

"Will you stop reading my notes?" she said as I flipped to a random page.

"Of course." I closed the book and grabbed another one.

"Abhi! Quit it! Those are personal!" She gasped when I turned to a random page. "Not that one! Please, not that one!"

Personal? This is what she reads? This is a whole bunch of NSFW shit. There's smut in this house!

"I'm dead," she whispered loud enough for me to hear.

I was intrigued. She doesn't seem like the type of person that would read this. "Care to explain?"

"I liked the plot. I usually skip over those scenes. That's why there's no highlighting, tabs, or notes," she answered.

I studied her for a bit. I could easily tell if she was lying to me, but she wasn't, so I turned to another page.

"Quit it! Give it back! We have an important issue to deal with."

To mess with her, I began reading the highlighted part, aloud. It was a scene where the guy was faking a proposal in front of others to make it look like it was a love marriage when it wasn't.

"Abhi."

That voice didn't belong to my wife.

I looked up from the book to see Nancy and Neeti grab the book right then and there.

"Yes?" I asked, grabbing Neeti before she could run away.

"Ishaan is asking if you could go to the hospital. Ellie is going, but he said you should come because their daughter lost a lot of blood, and your blood group matches."

"Tell him I'll be there right away. I'll take Ellie with me, since she can't drive."

Nancy nodded and left.

I turned to Neeti. "Sorry, I have to cut this short. I'll read all your notes when I come back."

"Just go. I will check on Riya. It's best if she doesn't find out yet. She's already shaken up. Please keep me updated, and take care of yourself. You suck at that."

"I will," I said, giving her a soft kiss and using the distraction to take the book back.

"I'm going to need someone to come with me!" I told her, running to get Ellie and leaving.

Varun

Why did Ellie and Abhi run out? What the hell is going on? We can't let Riya know. We can't let her see anything.

Neeti and Nancy were in the room with us again. They had both gone to check on their husbands and give us two the personal space we need.

I think without having to ask them, they were already on the same page as me. The problem was I couldn't understand why Riya asked why Ellie had to leave.

"Ishaan got a flat tire, so they both went," Neeti said. "Abhi will probably yell at him. He's always told Ishaan that he needs to learn that for whenever it happens."

Nice excuse.

"I see. Varun doesn't know how to change a flat tire either."

Way to throw me under the bus. At least Riya was smiling when she said it, so I didn't mind. *As long as she's smiling.*

She added, "He doesn't cook either. He goes to Vihaan's place for food when he's hungry, or I'll have something made for him."

She looked over at me, smiling. She was enjoying this, and I pretended to be irritated.

"What else? I think that's it. Do your husbands cook?" she asked.

Both of them nodded.

"What irritates you both? Like one thing you wish they'd stop doing? For me, it's snoring," Riya said, and I was sure I wanted to leave.

Nancy answered, "Being overprotective. I have to tell him where I am going, and then when I am leaving from there, I have to tell him my ETA. Don't get me wrong, I feel that Ryan is the best thing that happened to me, but it can be a lot at times."

"Trust me. I know," Riya said and told them about the whole texting situation while she was with Mia.

"I was worried!" I defended and turned to Neeti. "What about you?"

She shook her head. "I think we got used to each other. We have an enemies-to-lover story where he was in love the whole time but pretended he wasn't. I won't get too into it because that is a whole book on its own."

She paused before adding, "But there's something really nice about being with someone that makes you feel at peace and ensures you don't relive the abuse of the past again: safety."

Riya looked towards me, and when our eyes met, she said, "Trust me. I know that feeling a hundred percent."

Vihaan

Chapter 21

Two weeks later I had started to let the breakup go. Why was I even holding on for so long? She was getting married to someone else so be it. I will find someone else too if that's the case. Apparently, it didn't hurt her as much as it hurt me probably because I am the one that fell in love first.

"Chef, we have a customer that keeps asking for french toast. I told them it's not on the menu but they won't listen," August, told me.

I finally got my loans paid off where I had enough stuff to get orders out even faster than before. Unfortunately, what he said reminded me of Anaya and the first thing she told me when she ate at my restaurant.

"Kick them out," I almost commanded.

I changed the menu so none of her favorite items would be on present. I don't need my passion reminding me of her during every order.

"Yes chef!"

I, also, don't want anyone reminding me of someone I am trying to forget. I don't care if that means losing money because I would rather take the loss of that over my mental health. Whoever says men don't get hurt in breakups probably never loved someone the way that I did.

"Chef, they told me to give this to you," August handed me a piece of paper. I took it and shoved it into my pocket. There is no need to distract myself during the busiest hours I have.

"Hello brother," Esha smiled as she walked in. "Varun has requested hourly updates so I will be here watching you, reading your face and sending him the details. There was a time in my life that I did not like that man for what he did and now I think you are lucky enough to have him as your best friend. Can't relate."

"Of course he would tell you that now," I sighed and got to work. She opened her laptop and began typing away. She should make a bullet journal for my mood and behavior at this rate, at least it will be a pretty little photo Varun gets.

I pushed the fact Esha was here out of my mind and focused only on the dishes I was sending out. Varun sends Esha on the busiest days and I had to doubt several times if he gets footage from the cameras to him, even when Ryan had assured me that was not the case. Only Ryan and his people were getting access to everything and we still had no idea who Ryan's people were. His brother and him had a nice bond now that was beautiful to see. There were times Abhi would work while Ryan was watching a game with us and Abhi would fall asleep on his shoulder. It was heartwarming to know what Ryan had done for his brother.

The last of the dishes came back before I locked up for the night. All of us went through the back door anyway, so once everything was cleaned, all the dishes were done, floors mopped and broomed, we were ready to call it a night.

"And we are now going home," Esha spoke out what she was texting to Varun. I really don't need a babysitter, let alone two babysitters. I am completely fine! There is nothing wrong with me anymore and I need them to see that so they can quit watching me all the time. Varun still hasn't bought me the yacht. He really can't be doing this to me, I find it to be very unfair. How dare he babysit me and I get nothing out of it? I am going to demand my yacht from him.

At home I was changing when the paper fell out. I recognized the writing as Anaya's which meant that it was her earlier today. I told him to kick Anaya out and now I am sitting here having mixed feelings about that.

I would really appreciate it if we could talk. I will wait here until closing because I can see it's very busy. If you happen to see this afterwards I will wait at the park where we first got to know each other better, for an hour after your closing time. If you don't want to see me then I'll get the hint and never bother you again, but until then I will wait. In the hope that you could give me the chance to explain everything to you.

An hour after closing time? I even closed late today and nobody informed me that she was still waiting! I thought I said to kick her out. I hate how kind-hearted August is sometimes. I put the note on my desk as I grabbed my things to head out. I told myself the only reason I am doing this is because I deserved some sort of closure. It would be the last time I see or speak to her.

I arrived at the park and found her sitting alone. Is she stupid? Does she know she could get hurt waiting here alone this late? Does she not see how dark it is? She should have at least bought a jacket? She's going to catch a fucking cold.

I cleared my throat to make her aware of my presence.

"Hey chef," she greeted.

That hurt. She was the one that called me chef as a nickname and I always thought it was cute. I never did mind it until a few seconds ago when it made me feel as if she shot into my heart with one word.

"You do not get to call me that anymore," I told her, keeping my cool. I don't need people thinking I came all this way to yell at someone in a park. They would call the cops thinking I was some insane person.

"Right," she said with a controlled smile. "Do you want to sit?"

"No. I want you to tell me whatever it is you need to tell me so we can go our own ways."

"Okay. I know you heard what happened in California and I flew back here to talk to you because I really had no other reason to be back. What you heard was true," she said.

Fucking love that for me.

She continued, "However, it is against my will. I am being forced to marry someone because my mom found out what happened when Amber decided to pay the doctor. Varun took legal action and the doctor Amber paid has lost his license. My mom wouldn't believe me so she is getting me married off to some OB in training in the hopes that he will magically fix me. I don't need to be fixed. I really thought my family would be supportive and understanding but instead this is what is happening in Oregon at the moment. When I asked for the breakup, I did it because I had told my sister I don't get periods anymore on the phone and she told my mom. I didn't want you to have to deal with any of the backlash. You know how it is as a brown girl you are expected to be married and have kids or you failed. I should have picked the hints up when mom was always trying to get me to do something about the infertility issue. My blindass thought she was doing it to help the pain. Brown mom's don't give a fuck about the pain, as long as their daughter doesn't bring them shame. I wanted to tell you the truth that you deserved to hear. They have no idea I am even meeting up with you since I said it's just a get together with my east coast friends."

I heard her whisper, "Plus you are the last person I wanted to see."

Anaya and I had even discussed adopting kids prior to the breakup. I had known her situation since I was the one that took her to the hospital that night. I began to save up money without her even knowing as soon as we both knew we wanted to adopt and be with each other. I still have that money saved up and added to it after the breakup, in the hope she would come back someday. Now she is here and I have no idea what to do.

"I really am sorry. I know I hurt you but the goal was to not let you suffer any of the backlash."

With simple directness I said, "What did you mean by the last person I wanted to see? I have a feeling from everything you said already and I really hope I am wrong."

It wasn't hard to do the math and notice she wanted to end her life rather than get married to someone against her will to portray an image to society. Unfortunately, I was right. Why does she do this? When I want to be wrong, I am right and vice versa.

"Where are you staying in Jersey?" I asked as light rain began to fall.

"A hotel. I told them I would and they were tracking my credit card."

"How are you getting around? You sold your car before moving back."

"Rideshare."

"Food?" I had to ask because she hates cooking. I thought it balanced our relationship out quite well at the time. Girlfriend who hates cooking and boyfriend who's a chef. I would happily do all the cooking for her because I enjoyed it.

"I have money for food, Vihaan. This isn't important right now, what is important is you getting the closure you need. Riya told me everything! I never meant to hurt you to the point you lost yourself. You have Varun getting updates on you because he is worried you might hurt yourself," she now had tears going down but still spoke in her perpetually tired voice. "Please don't do this to yourself."

"You know how apologizes work Anaya. I don't have to forgive you and you know the reason why."

I began to believe in Anaya's reasons for apologizing for the longest time until she was the one that shattered my heart into bite size pieces.

"I know but you still deserved to know the truth."

Funny how I was thinking the truth would have hurt a lot less while in California but now that I know it, it sure as hell hurts a lot more. She lied to me so she can deal with all the consequences on her own. She wanted me to be the last person she saw before she ended everything and took her life. She flew out here just so I could know the truth face to face, when Riya probably told her that I didn't block her number waiting for a call to explain everything.

"I should head back to the hotel now. Thank you for coming to see me and you already know I only would ever wish you the best," she said, getting up and walking away.

A moment of reflection before I asked, "Then why is the best I ever had walking away?"

That got her to stop in her tracks. I ran over to catch up with her because I wasn't letting her walk away this time. I did that already did once and that shit was painful as fuck.

"Answer me please. I need to know why you are walking away," I said.

"Vihaan, you just said that you don't have to accept my apology. Why would I not walk away if that is the case?"

"I did say that but you have to let me finish. I don't have to accept your apology but it would be very painful if I didn't. Yes, I was hurt by what happened because I didn't know the truth. I thought knowing it would hurt less but knowing you did that so I wouldn't get the short end of the stick hurts more. You suffered alone and never told anyone. I would have known if Riya knew. Riya tells Varun and Varun forwards it to me. I am handcuffing you to me this time so you better get used to my presence in your life. There is no way you are going back to Oregon after everything you told me. I'll tell Ryan to get his people to keep an eye on you as well if I have to," I said before giving her a kiss.

I missed her so much! I made sure our kiss was deep and passionate. We had to make up for all the days we didn't get to kiss.

I took her back to the hotel where I would be spending the night with her, but first I had to video call Riya and Varun to see their reactions. Anaya said she would be out of the frame just to hear what they say. Plus, Varun owes me for babysitting me. I get what he did because he cares, but hourly updates are a lot so he deserves what I'm about to do to him.

"Hel- that is not your room or your house. Sir, where the hell are you?" Varun asked as soon as answered. Riya joined a few seconds later.

I rolled my eyes when he said *sir* because he knows I hate that. All the more reason to mess with him.

"Hi bhabi!"

"You sound happy," she smiled. "That's good but where are you?"

"In a hotel room," I shrugged as I answered.

"Why are you in a hotel room?" Varun stressed the question. I could even see the stress on his face as he asked.

"So you know how I was trying to get over my breakup?" I asked.

With a gloomy sigh Varun said, "You did not sleep with another woman! Please tell me you did not sleep with someone. This is why you were being watched! Where is my phone? Oh, I am using it! I am going to ask Esha what she missed. Vihaan, we went over healthy ways to get over a breakup. I am going to have a heart attack any second. What part of healthy did you not understand? Healthy without the letters u and n in front of the word."

Still no off button I see. I had to hide my smile because I was on camera but Anaya was doing her best not to laugh.

"There is a woman in the room," I said just to see how much worse it could get.

"Vihaan!" He yelled at me. Oh shit, he's serious now. "That's it! I am flying back to the east coast because apparently you can't be trusted. Did you just go for someone that threw themselves at you? Is that what you're doing now? You are letting the rumors that started after your breakup with

Camren come true? I get that you are an adult but come on! I can't believe I am going to have to tell you this but Anaya loves you. She never stopped loving your stupid ass."

"At least mine isn't flat," I cut him off to say.

He didn't have any of my shit, "Really jokes? You have time to sleep around and make jokes! Listen asshole! Anaya went back to the east coast to see you so she can tell you everything. You have to give her a chance to hear what she has to say. It is very important that you know."

"I know," I admitted.

"I don't know when she is going to tell you -did you just say I know?" He asked as Anaya came into the frame.

"Hello friends," she smiled and both of us began laughing.

"You almost gave him a heart attack! You should see how fast his pulse is," Riya exclaimed. "Good to see you both together."

"I had to mess with him for babysitting me."

"I was worried," Varun defended. "Fucking asshole!"

After a few minutes of catching up I asked them about elopements. They had eloped due to circumstances and looks like we would have to do the same. They answered any question we had by comparing circumstances. We probably spent over an hour just discussing eloping before calling it a night. I had called home to let them know I wouldn't be coming and there was no need to update Varun since he knew. If they don't stop babysitting now, I am going to be very upset.

"I'm going to be in a boatload of trouble when everyone back home finds out," Anaya said.

"It's a good thing you don't have to go back there."

"I work there. I sold everything I had prior to moving to Oregon, so I literally don't have anything here except the shit I packed."

It's a good thing I earned more over these years. I am sure that mom and Esha won't have a problem sharing anything once I tell them the situation I landed myself in again. I really do end up landing myself in something when it comes to her. I have enough money saved up as well that we could start buying anything she needed, that wouldn't come out of the adoption funds.

"Just put your notice in saying you aren't coming back. Don't even give them two weeks because they don't deserve to know that. Say bye-bye."

"And exactly how do you expect me to find another job here?" She questioned in response.

"Who said you have to work?" I asked, showing how much money I had managed to save up.

"I am working regardless. Now, we have to think about how your mom is going to react to the situation we are in."

"I have a feeling she will be completely fine with it," I said because I know my mom and there wasn't a chance she wouldn't be.

Vihaan

Chapter 22

"Beautiful, are you ready yet?" I asked again.

This is now the fifth time I have had to ask. I could have toured our entire hotel in New Zealand by now.

I need to think of something else I could do because I've scrolled through my phone, called Varun, and my mom thought of new menu items and my wife still wasn't ready.

Anaya and I decided on having an elopement ceremony two months ago that everyone we met in California, Varun, Riya, Esha and my mom could attend.

I stayed in touch with the photographer who took my restaurant opening photos and invited him back for the

Michelin star photos and he called me a few months prior, inviting me to the birthday party for his twins. I had no idea I even had kids. He never posted their birth, milestones or anything.

"I'm ready," Anaya finally said. She had on a simple pastel yellow Indian outfit. There was no design on the top or bottom, but the floral dupatta was the main point.

She really makes simple look beautiful.

"You took so long," I complained.

"Sorry, not all of us were born as perfect as you, Mr. Vihaan Armani."

"You think I'm perfect? Good to know. I'll hold it against you if you ever think I'm not, Mrs. Anaya Armani."

She didn't say anything to that. She probably got used to me calling her by our last name in these months.

We left for the venue while she kept saying I wasn't perfect and she only said to boost my ego. It worked! My ego was completely boosted.

I hadn't seen Rohan in years. He looked so different but yet still the same. He was the best photographer I have ever worked with. I wanted him to capture the elopement ceremony because I wanted those photos to show to our children whenever we adopted them. I messaged him on Instagram, only for him to tell me he had moved to New Zealand. How private does he keep his life, was my first thought when he told me. He still flew out to take them without me even having to offer double. I was typing I would pay double, but he agreed before I could press send.

"Hey! You made it!" Rohan happily greeted me.

"Well, you made it to New Jersey for me. Returning the favor."

"I do not miss the States, but I do miss your food. You bring any with you?" He asked.

"It would've been ruined," I stated the obvious before a child, who I assumed from the eyes, was his daughter, joined us.

"I'll have to come back to the States then. Just for you. I hardly go anymore because Mari moved to Australia with her family. She was the only reason I had to ever go."

"Well, less flight time for you. I'm assuming this is your daughter?"

He nodded, "One of my beautiful angels. This one is calmer. My son is a loud mess, but I love him."

He told her to say hi to us and she sweetly waved. Rohan told us to head inside since it was getting colder.

He really loves his kids. There was no way anyone couldn't see that. They both stuck with him more than their mom throughout the party.

My phone kept vibrating as I talked to Anaya about what I had planned for the week we would be here.

Why am I not surprised? I showed it to my wife, who simply laughed seeing the name.

VARUN - I miss you 😔

VARUN - a week away. How will my heart handle it?

VARUN - don't you miss me?

VARUN - you got a wife and forgot about me💔

VARUN - send pics of New Zealand 🇳🇿

VARUN - your assistant chef is good 👍

VARUN - but it's not you 😭

VARUN - I see you reading these 😄

VIHAAN - I am going to block you 😒

VARUN - you did that once. For several months. Bad times

VIHAAN - you did that to yourself 😑

VARUN - how's bhabi?

VIHAAN- she's good. Making friends. I should do that! Maybe I can find a best friend here. Move here and forget you exist

VARUN - 🖕

I laughed as I put my phone away. I'll show Anaya this conversation later. She knows Varun can't survive without me. Riya went to Paris with Neeti for a fashion show. Since he knew his wife was busy he kept calling or texting me as if I wasn't.

"Chef, do you want some food?" Anaya asked.

"We're married now. Stop calling me chef! You can call me hubby instead."

"Sir, would you like something to put inside your stomach?" She asked instead.

"I hate you," I laughed.

I could never hate the most beautiful consequence of my life.

"Do you, now? Didn't seem to be the case regarding last night and this morning."

I spit my drink out. I was not expecting her to say that out in public. Granted, nobody could hear us but still.

"In my defense, you agreed to let this double be a honeymoon," I said, cleaning up the mess.

"I'll remember you hate me then. I'll just honeymoon alone. Maybe I'll find a good-looking man on one of these beaches."

"Don't even think about it."

"Thought about it!"

Is it possible to return your wife? Ship here right back to Oregon? Just kidding! I wouldn't ever let her go through that.

When she posted our wedding photos on social media, her phone went off nonstop from her family. We discussed why she wanted to post it and the consequences. She said she's happy to be my wife, so she wants to. Her family was not thrilled about what we had done. She was getting cussed out, threatened and being called names such as a slut and whore, simply because she chose happiness over society. People even questioned her on if we slept together or if she was pregnant pre-marriage, causing her to elope. Our first time was almost two months into our wedding, but people kept saying she was probably pregnant or something. They blamed her for the elopement. It got to the point where I started answering calls and telling me to talk to me instead. I talked back! I wasn't going to let society pressure her into anything she didn't want. Nor was I going to tell people that she couldn't have kids. Whatever happens in our lives will solely be based on what we want. Nobody else will ever matter.

"What're you thinking about? I've said your name three times," Anaya's voice took me out of my thoughts.

Just to mess with her I said, "I was thinking about cuddling. There's no guest room you can escape to here."

She lit up as she laughed, remembering our old conversations, "Idiot."

We really came so far in our relationship. I'm definitely not going to let anyone take her away from me.

Avani and Rohan had taken their twins to cut the cake. I'll be honest, I haven't had cake in so long! The last birthday party I went to was Amber's unfortunate party. Come to think of it, that led to Anaya and I breaking up the first time. That time she did it because she didn't want to break my trust by breaking a rule. The second time she did it, she didn't want anyone to say or do anything to me. She was always looking out for me. Now, if she asks for a divorce,

I'll ensure we get the word never tattooed on her, so she'll remember I'm not letting her fight alone.

We had birthday celebrations with cookie cakes or cupcakes. Nobody wanted to get an entire cake since only a few of us were there.

I can't wrap my head around the fact his twins were five years old. It's a kid's party, but there's alcohol at least.

"You can't drink. You've already tried to drink your way to death so you lost your privilege," Avani said when I told her I was going to the bar. "Riya tells me everything."

"To be fair, I thought it would make the breakup hurt less, but since you are saying it with concern, I'll sit this one out."

This cake was so good! A vanilla cake with salted caramel buttercream frosting. Not as good as the hokey pokey ice cream we had earlier, but it's definitely a close second for dessert. Although, we have yet to try pavlova, pineapple lumps, and the various lollies. I hope I get some dessert inspiration, at least. The only problem is I probably won't be able to make it as good.

After we ate and said our goodbyes, it was back to the hotel. Rohan offered to take us around, but I didn't want to be a burden. He said he wouldn't mind, so now we have him taking us around tomorrow. I'll be fine with it if he brings his wife, so mine doesn't get bored.

"I'm so exhausted," Avani said as we walked into the room. "I don't have the energy to do my skincare routine."

I faked a gasp, "The day has finally come when Avani doesn't do skincare!"

She threw the pillow at me.

"Missed me, wifey!"

"I'm going to kill you."

"We'll see about that," I smirked. "You love me too much."

"Unfortunately."

"At least you admitted it," I said as I thought to myself *I win.*

Chapter 23

I woke up to the sound of dishes clattering and TV. It seemed that everyone was awake. I could barely open my eyes and would love to doze off again and get just a few more minutes of sleep.

We had moved into our new place, even though I told Varun it would be okay to live with my in-laws after we adopted our kids. We intended to adopt only one child, but when we found out that he had a sister, Varun suggested that we adopt them both. We didn't like the idea of separating a brother and sister. They had already lost their parents and were the only family each other had. How cruel would it be of us to only take one?

Our daughter, Elle, was only six months and our son, Leo, was three when we adopted them. Their mother and father had left them out and someone found them. I was watching the news about them being abandoned in a park and quickly called Varun, asking if we could adopt them. He wouldn't say no to me, but this was a big step. After what felt like ages, we finally brought them home.

With our daughter crying at night, Varun brought up moving out with his parents and they didn't mind the cries. He, however, thought it was for the best. Without me knowing, he signed the papers and bought us a home. We've been living here for the past eight months now.

Our home is a single floor with four bedrooms, three bathrooms, a backyard big enough to have someone host their wedding, a living room and a kitchen with wood floors. He has childproofed the whole place to make it easy for the kids.

Anaya and Vihaan have started the paperwork for their adoption journey as well. I'm so happy and excited for them. Our best friends will have our kids be best friends too!

I should get my lazy ass out of bed and shower. Varun won't care what time I wake up. I could sleep until 3 PM if I wanted to. He's an amazing husband and dad. He takes care of his family so well. If I thought my safety was a concern, he's even more worried about the kids. He'll kick them out if anyone breathes the wrong way around them. He's changed his hours so now he works 7 AM to 3 PM whereas he used to work 9 AM to 5 PM, to have more time with all of us. He didn't need to since I worked from home now, but he said he didn't want to miss anything.

I lazily dragged myself into the shower and took care of my daily morning routine.

Everyone was watching Saturday morning cartoons while Varun fed our daughter. Leo was having his half cup of cereal. They had yet to notice me entering.

It warmed my heart to see my family together. My family! I never thought I'd be alive long to refer to someone else as my family. I love this family more than anything else. Definitely better than the family I grew up with.

"Momma!" Leo finally noticed me.

I smiled at him from my spot before giving him a big hug. He was older when they were abandoned, so the word mom or any form of it took him so long to say.

When he finally did call me mom, I couldn't express the joy it had bought me.

"You had your breakfast?" I asked both him and Varun.

"Yes," they both replied.

"I'll make you breakfast, Riya. Just let me finish here," Varun told me.

Oh, that reminds me, I'm no longer his princess. I'm simply Riya now because he calls Elle his princess instead.

"I'll get it, Varun," I said, earning a look questioning why I added his name.

He's not dumb, though. He turned his attention fully on our daughter, "You see. Mommy is jealous that you're my princess now. My beautiful princess. You have a little more left. Almost done. Then we can go to the park."

Rude! I am not jealous! How dare he lie to Elle like that.

"It's okay, mommy. I love you," Leo said. "Even if dad doesn't. What does jealousy mean?"

I hugged him again. "Jealousy means green with envy. I love you too."

"Is that why the cartoons turn green when they puke?"

"No, this has nothing to do with puking. It has everything to do with your dad being a jerk."

"Daddy is not a jerk! He doesn't leave us outside alone for a long time," he said, breaking my heart. What could we do to make him forget that? I couldn't even imagine how he felt being left out in the dark and cold for so long. "He's nice. He buys us nice things and loves us. And he keeps us warm. And he bought us a home. And he loves you, mommy!"

I smiled at him before looking over at Varun. There was something in his eyes that for the first time, I couldn't read.

"I love all of you," Varun said. "That's correct."

Our doorbell went off right as I got up to get some breakfast.

"Hi, Vihaan. You came alone?" I asked, opening the door and not seeing Anaya.

He doesn't look good. Something is wrong because the last time he was this broken was when Anaya broke up with him. I invited him without saying another word and Leo ran to him.

That brought a smile to his face. Vihaan and Leo were more like besties than Varun and Vihaan.

One look and Varun asked, "What's wrong?"

I should probably take the kids away from this.

"Anaya," was all Vihaan said and I put everything down. Please don't tell me they broke up again. Well, it would be divorce now, but still. I don't want to hear that. I'll fight her.

He turned towards Varun, "I feel horrible asking you for this, but could I borrow some money? Anaya's family beat her senseless when she went back to Oregon. I spent almost everything I had on her bill because her insurance didn't go through and we also paid some fees in the adoption process. I told her not to go back, but she said it's been years. She wants to make things right. I said I'd go with her, but she wanted me to watch the restaurant. I fucked up by not going along."

Vihaan was crying and I also had tears going down my face. I wiped them fast because I never wanted my kids to see me cry. I have to be strong for them.

"Vihaan," Varun said, taking Elle in his lap now that she was done eating. "You don't have to feel bad. I kind of owe you my life, remember?"

"I'll pay you back. I promise."

"Then I'm not giving you any. I'll only give it if you promise to not pay me back. You helped out when Riya was in a similar situation."

Leo gasped. "Mom got beat up? I'll fight them. I'm small, but I'm very strong."

I couldn't help but think back to when Varun and I first discussed having children. The day he bought me my polaroid camera back as an excuse to see me.

"Mommy's all good and strong now," Varun told him. "Do you want to go watch TV?"

Leo nodded. Perfect timing since his favorite cartoon was on. Once Varun got our son distracted it was back to the conversation.

"Is Anaya still in Oregon?" I couldn't help but ask.

Vihaan nodded. "She couldn't make it back here with how horribly messed up she looks. I couldn't see the photos. I just want to be with my wife. I don't care if I lose my restaurant. Hell, I don't care if I lose my star. Nothing can make me happier than being by her side right now."

"Vihaan, you know I would go with you. Elle, really still doesn't go through a night without waking up. I can't take her on a plane," Varun said, but I stopped him.

"He will go with you. I'll take care of the kids without a problem. Plus, we have my in-laws. Anaya is important to all of us. He's going and that's final," I grabbed my phone off the table. "I know someone else that can help."

I searched for Abhi's number and called him to have his wife answer. I started with small talk because it was way too awkward to ask for a favor immediately.

"Ah, Abhi is here," she said. I heard her tell him I was on the phone.

"Did you get in trouble again?" Abhi asked, taking his phone.

"I may need a small favor," I emphasized the word may.

"Do you need a private jet or some money?"

"You have a private jet?!"

He really knows how money works. No wonder his company hasn't tanked yet.

"I told Ryan, 'what would it cost for you to stop reminding me daily of what you did for Neeti and me?' This lovely brother of mine joked around and said private jet, so I bought one. Did you hear Nancy's pregnant? Mia probably already told you. I'm so excited! I'm going to embarrass the hell out of Ryan when his kid gets older. Oh, I'm blabbering."

Ryan and Nancy would make such great parents. We definitely need another trip to California when we get a chance. The question becomes what would we take as a present? When he found out we had kids, Ryan sent me a ten thousand dollar check. He said it's because adoption is expensive, which it is, but it was mostly so we can buy the kids whatever they wanted or save up for their college fees. Abhi and Mia also sent a bunch of toys and money. The kids probably had college covered simply since I was related to Mia. Whatever we took wouldn't be enough.

"Actually, a private jet would be helpful. How much would it cost to borrow that?" I asked.

"Mia would murder me for charging her cousin a penny. It's free for family and staying alive purposes."

I laughed before explaining the situation. He told us where to go and he would have someone bring us to Oregon and fly us back whenever needed. He was going to cover the cost of the hotel without me asking for money. He offered to cover as much as the bill required.

"Thank you. We all really appreciate it," I said.

"Please don't thank me. I'm glad to put my money towards something that isn't building another library or books."

A pause before he goes, "Ow!"

I knew Neeti would hurt him for saying that. Their enemies-to-lovers love story is my favorite.

I hung up the call after getting confirmation that someone was already on their way. I told the guys what would happen and what Abhi had offered.

"He bought his brother a private jet to shut him up?" Varun asked.

I nodded.

"My brother would just make it worse. Unfair."

The guys left for the location Abhi sent about three hours after the phone call. Varun sent me a text when they arrived there, told me that Mia's husband, Joshua, was with them, then texted me again when they arrived in Oregon and then when they got to the hospital.

Anaya's strong. She's going to be okay. She has to be okay.

"Mommy, is everything okay? Is dad going to come back?" Leo asked.

I blinked away my tears. "Yes. In a few days, he'll be home. Everything is fine."

He nodded before turning back to his show.

Everything is fine because it has to be.

Vihaan

Varun was the only one with me. Joshua went back to California after attending some business in Oregon of his own.

I only saw the photos of Anaya. The last time she was in the hospital was because Varun was blackmailed into doing so.

"Family?" I was asked by a staff member.

I nodded. "Husband, and he's her brother-in-law."

I didn't have a real brother. I always considered Varun to be that, so that technically does make him her brother-in-law.

After doing some paperwork, she let us in. We walked inside and I immediately wanted to find those people and dislocate every bone in their bodies.

She wanted them to talk things out and be a family like they used to be, but she was almost beaten to death. I won't ever forgive them.

"You want to be alone?" Varun asked.

I didn't know if I did. I wish I knew if she was responsive. When I got the call from her emergency contact that she was hospitalized, I immediately didn't know what to do. I had so many mixed emotions, but I was on the opposite side of the country.

A doctor walked in before I could answer. We introduced ourselves to her. She told us that Anaya was awake and responding. She did have several bruises and a broken arm.

I will break each person's arm that did that to her.

The doctor said the medicine should be wearing off soon and she'll be awake. She added it was nice to see someone visit her since nobody dropped by. I explained the long-distance situation while Varun stepped out, saying he would see what he could do about the bill.

I waited for her to wake up, taking her hand in mine. I had to move the stool to the opposite side so it wasn't her broken side I was holding.

Forty minutes passed by before I heard her say my name.

"How are you feeling?" I asked.

"Why did you come here?"

Is she crazy? Last time I thought it was the smoke this time, I think the drugs are going to her head.

"Because I love you and you're my wife."

"I know," she laughed a little. "But you'll lose your star with how many days it will take you here."

I don't care. I moved so I could kiss her. It's been a week since I last saw, held or kissed. I was sure to make this kiss worth the entire week we missed, but why is she tapping on my arm like I have her in a submission hold and she has to tap out.

Oh shit! Oxygen! I pulled away as soon as I realized that.

"Good kisser, green flag," she started again. I couldn't help but laugh.

The last time Anaya was in a hospital, our real relationship. That was the end of us fake-dating.

"I love you, Anaya. I love you so much. I don't care if I lose my star or my restaurant. That was something I wanted. You're something I need. I need to have you by my side to be able to survive. I can't sleep, eat or think when you aren't around. I told you not to go or to have me come with you. I will make them pay for this. Trust me."

I give her a soft kiss this time.

"I won't be able to call you chef if you lose that," she joked.

"Beautiful, we agreed you won't call me that anymore, regardless."

"We did? When? Was I there?"

I roll my eyes at that. She should call me hubby instead now. Chef was cute when we were fake dating or even during the dating stages, but I'm her husband now.

"Varun!" She cheerfully greeted him as he walked in. She turned to me, adding, "Look, you bought a friend."

"How are you feeling?" Varun asked.

"My arm hurts. Shit's broken, apparently. How are you? How's Riya? Is she here? How are the kids? I miss the kids!"

"We're all good. They're back home in New Jersey. Afraid you get us two only."

"Having some company is better than none. What about your patients, though?"

"Oh, I'm flying back early morning. I got myself an Uber and a flight ticket. Your lovely husband here will take you back on a private jet."

Anaya tried her best to sit up upon hearing that. I helped her the best I could. Still determining how comfortable she was.

I told my wife about everything Abhi did for us and how Varun was here to help me pay the bill.

"That's a lot of money to pay back. Will you take payments?" She asked Varun.

"You know what. I will," he said. I thought he didn't want the money back. "Give me a guy's night with my best friend once a month. We'll call it even."

I had to bite my tongue from laughing. I really have him as a best friend.

"Can you keep him?" Anaya asked.

The audacity! What did I do? Breath wrong?

"I would love to, but I already have two kids. Riya and I are happy with two. A third isn't in the picture."

"Asshole," I say to him.

"Sir, can you please not call my guest an asshole," Anaya almost commanded.

Introducing these two was a horrible idea. Varun rubbed off on her. Hate it.

He was laughing away, "She called you. sir!"

Hilarious. Why don't you gang up on me while you're at it? I should listen to Riya. Lots of wine and yoga will get me through this.

"That reminds me of this one time in high school," Varun started.

This can't go well. Who needs enemies when your best friend exists?

He continued, "Vihaan decided that he would walk around the school and someone who was subbing that day thought he was staff. They went, "Sir, do you know how I can find this classroom,' That's when I started calling him sir. He looks older than he is. He's lucky to have landed you."

I love that Anaya was laughing because laughter is the best medicine. Still, I wish it didn't cost my embarrassing stories.

Varun probably told her every embarrassing thing that has happened to me since elementary school until now. I'm sitting here thinking how much someone would buy him for. 70 cents? Free? A dollar?

Riya video called to check in on Anaya and because the kids, well Leo, wanted to say hi.

I took the opportunity to look at my wife. Her bruises and her arm will, too, according to the doctors. How long will it take for her to heal from the trauma she now has to suffer? How long before she gets the glow in her eyes back? How long before she's not faking a smile? How long before I remind her she can cry in front of me? She doesn't need to bottle it up.

Varun had left about an hour afterward to catch his flight.

"Vihaan," she said, taking my hand. "Thank you for coming across the country for me."

"This is nothing. I'd go all the way across the globe for you on foot. I love you."

"I love you too, chef. I always will, so you are stuck with me for a lifetime and I know all your embarrassing stories. What's the deal? Will you still stay?"

I pretend to sigh just to hear her laugh.

"I'll always stay beautiful. How can I not when I don't know any embarrassing things about you? Can't leave without an even score."

She laughed again. Music to my ears. "Good luck, chef. You most definitely will need it."

Vihaan

Chapter 24

New Zealand has to have shown me the craziest rainstorm of my life. I live on America's east coast, but this will have to be in my record books. We came back to New Zealand almost a month after Anaya was doing better, because she missed the country.

Rohan had come to pick us up today since he offered to show us around. I had told him we'd get a ride to his place, but he took the drive over instead. Thanks to the weather, we weren't going out anywhere.

He had to step away because his parents needed something. I didn't mind. I enjoyed teaching his twins how to bake. They had a cute little baking set and we were making sugar cookies. They really were creative kids from everything I have seen and been told.

"I'll put them in the oven. You both will have to wait," I said when we were done.

Didn't need kids going anywhere near there. It's going to be about twelve minutes until the cookies are ready.

Avani and Anaya seemed busy in what looked like a really important conversation. What if she's thinking about moving to New Zealand?

That just gave me an idea. I grabbed my phone from the table and texted Varun.

Vihaan - so Anaya really likes it here. We're thinking of moving 🤔

Varun - buy a house with a spare room for me to live in. Bold if you to assume I wouldn't follow your ass there

Vihaan - what if I'm moving to get away from you

Varun - I'll have someone track you down 😑

Varun - you can't leave your restaurant 😝

Vihaan - I could relocate here

Varun read that message but never replied. Instead, Anaya's phone went off and she looked over at me.

"You want me to answer it?" I asked and she nodded.

It must be an earnest conversation. I wonder what it's about. She'll tell me later and if she doesn't, I'll just tickle her until she does.

"Hel-"

Varun spoke before I could even finish. "You can't move to New Zealand! If you do, can you divorce Vihaan? Send him back to me. I'll help you find someone even better than him! He'll be even more handsome than Vihaan! Please! Can you drop him off? I'll pick him up at the airport."

"I'm not letting my wife divorce me for you. It was a joke, but I have thought about replacing you several times," I said as I checked on the cookies.

In California and here, the three kids I've met have to be the most well-behaved. The twins returned to their coloring pages and patiently waited for the timer to go off.

"Don't you dare replace me! I won't allow it."

Rohan walked in drenched and even though this was his house, I felt I should offer to make him something warm instead.

"I'll talk to you later," I told Varun and hung up. I already knew from our friendship that whatever he was going to say next would just be nonsense.

"What's in the oven?" He asked.

"The twins wanted to play with the cookie cutters, so I offered to help them bake some sugar cookies."

He faked a gasp, "Do they know they worked with a Michelin star chef?"

"Shut it. I enjoyed doing this, actually. I never got to cook or bake with kids before." Realization dawned on me and I added. "Well, your kids are just well-behaved. I probably won't enjoy it with every kid."

"Avani did a great job raising them," he said, taking a seat further away, almost as if he didn't want the kids to hear. "Let me tell you something about relationships. Healthy relationships aren't fairytales. Healthy relationships are uncomfortable conversations and emotional vulnerability. People underestimate how much work goes into a relationship they just see photos of. You work for it."

He's right. Relationships aren't something people luck into. Every relationship has its ups and downs. The ones that survive are the ones someone fought for. Unless it turns into only one person fighting to keep it alive, then it's best to peace out.

"Why are you telling me this? I get that we're newly married, but I still know that much," I told him, confused as the timer went off.

I got the tray out and let the kids know we'd put icing once they cooled down. They both smiled and went to now playing tic-tac-toe with each other.

"I'm telling you because I don't want you to fuck up the way I did," he said, going into all the detail from the divorce to finding out about the twins to where they were now. Unfortunately, Anaya can't have kids, so that takes that part out. I wasn't going to tell him that, though. He may be a great friend, but my personal life was personal. Relationships don't survive if you air out everything.

I decided to change the subject. "Your kids get along well with each other. Who's the elder one?"

"Noor is. They're each other's best friends. Watch this," he said, calling Noah over and giving him half a cookie.

Noah broke that half and gave the other piece to his sister without anyone telling him.

"They share everything," Rohan smiled. "If you give one of something, say a lollipop and not the other, they'll give it back and wait until they both have one."

"That's beautiful. They learned to share from a young age," I said, checking to see if the cookies were cool enough for frosting.

"Avani and I have a joke that it's because they've been sharing since the womb."

I laughed at that since it was true. Twins do start sharing before birth.

I told the kids that it was time to put the frosting and they ran over-excited. Their dad told them to slow down before they got hurt.

I guided them on how to add frosting to anything, not just cookies. Hopefully, they'll remember it in the future. I let them have the cookies before offering them to everyone else and then take one for myself last.

We all spent time talking about any and everything, from the weather differences to property tax and health care.

"I think you should spend the night here instead of going back," Avani suggested pointing to the window.

The weather had gotten even worse. I had enough money to not care about the hotel room I was paying for, so I agreed. I should have double-checked first, but it seems Anaya didn't mind.

She looked at her phone, which was lighting up.

"Riya," she said as she excused herself.

Would it be wrong of me to ask Avani what they discussed earlier? Yes. I need to ask Anaya. I excused myself to let them have some time for themselves and their kids.

Rohan had already shown us where the guest room was. It was decent-sized with a full-size bed, two bedside tables with lamps, and a small ceiling fan that smelled like sandalwood.

"Hi bhabi," I said, joining the video call.

"Hey. How are you? Varun is freaking out that you're going to leave him," she laughed.

"Wouldn't be his first time. What were you both talking about?" I asked.

Anaya let me hold her phone while she snuggled closer.

"Nothing much. I was just telling her about the fashion show. I got back last night, so I had to inform my best friend."

Riya seemed so happy, as I congratulated her.

"Thank you."

Riya didn't say anything. She pointed at Anaya, who'd knocked out, to confirm if she had fallen asleep.

I nodded.

"Guess I'll have to talk to you both later then. Bye Vihaan," she said, but she couldn't hang up because Varun heard her say that and took the phone.

"Listen here, you asshole. You are getting on that plane and flying that lovely flat ass of yours back to the United States," he huffed.

"Bye!" I hung up the call immediately, putting the phone on airplane mode.

I turned to Anaya, who was peacefully asleep. She's stunning even while she's bare-faced. She'll only wake up if I try to take the ring on her finger off. It's surprising, honestly, because she's a deep sleeper until someone touches the ring.

The ring I'd given her was three carats, rose gold, marquise-shaped. Mom had offered to give her the wedding ring she had been proposed with, but I didn't want to do that. Mom suffered from an abusive relationship. I didn't need anything reminding me daily of that. I gathered the money to buy Anaya a ring on my own.

I felt at peace when we heard that dad had passed away. Knowing nothing would ever hurt my family now was the most peaceful news I could have ever received.

I didn't know what type of monster I'd become if anything happened to any family member.

Avani's phone vibrating made me realize that I had been staring at her the whole time. I can't help it. If you have a beautiful partner, you gaze lovingly.

What the fuck? This has to be some kind of joke. There's no way I just read the name mom on her phone. She should have them blocked by now, shouldn't she?

"Anaya," I tried to wake her up. "Babe."

No luck. I tried to lightly shake her, but she was out. Ya, we shouldn't have done anything last night. It's not my fault I can't get enough of her. She's beautiful.

"Anaya," I tried again.

The vibration was now replaced with her ringtone. Crap! One last try or I'll answer. "Anaya."

Well, I tried.

"Hello," I answered.

"Who are you? Are you the one that encouraged her to run away? Are you the one that married her without permission?" Her mom fired the questions.

Well, I'm not one to back down.

"Actually, I had permission. When I asked Anaya if she would marry me, she replied yes. Therefore, I didn't need to get toxic people involved. And one other thing, if you ever call my wife again to do anything that isn't apologizing, I won't have any of it," I warned.

"Give the phone to that woman. If she's going to elope, she can at least tell us when we'll have grandkids. Oh wait, she can't do that either."

I looked over at my wife. Nothing hurt us more than what Camren and that money-hungry doctor did to her.

"Anaya isn't available. Not now, not ever, especially for you people. If any of you tries to call her again, I'll have your bodies sent back to the family. Stay the fuck away from my wife. You lost your privileges to talk to her."

I hung up the call blocking the number. Why has she not blocked it? Was she waiting for an apology?

Anaya stretched her body as if waking up. I had so many questions to ask her.

"I fell asleep. See, this is why I don't trust you," she said, smiling, unaware of what had happened a few seconds ago.

"I can't help that you're beautiful. But anyways, what did you and Avani talk about?"

Her smile fell as soon as I asked.

What could be that detrimental?

"How people automatically assume things in the Brown community. Avani also went through it when she got divorced and I went through it with eloping. We both got looked down upon because we're the females," she stopped looking down to look at me. "That's why I consider myself lucky to have you. Your family, friends, and you don't judge me. I can be myself."

Now it makes even more sense why Rohan said not everything was as it seemed. I didn't even know about the divorce until he told me today. Now, I'm finding out that Avani also went through society being a bitch.

She placed her hand on my face before leaning in for a kiss.

"I love you, chef."

"I love you more. Just remember I fell in love first, so I can say that."

She chuckled. "I'm thankful I agreed to fake dating you. It led me to the most beautiful consequence of my life."

"Funny. I, too, call you the most beautiful consequence of mine."

Her smile was back. I missed it in the few seconds it wasn't present.

"We should go back outside," I said.

"One more kiss," she begged.

Okay, one more. But it wasn't one more. She kept saying one more again and again.

"Anaya, we have to stop. We're at someone's house and if we don't, I'm going to want to do something that isn't right to do in a friend's guest room," I warned her.

"Race you out," she said and almost flew out before I could even comprehend what had just happened.

She's lucky I love her. Very lucky.

Varun

Epilogue

"Leo, please finish eating. You can go hang out with the others when you're done," I said.

"Okay. We're going to the roller coasters today!"

"I'm aware," I told him as he quickly finished.

Vihaan was taking his daughter, Leo and Ash to the amusement park. Vihaan and Anaya adopted their daughter when she was three. Now both Leo and Ezra were seven years old. Although Leo had Elle, he never let Ezra feel like she was an only sibling.

"Can Elle come with us?" Leo asked again.

"Sorry, but she's still sick. You know I'd let her come if she wasn't."

"But you're a doctor. Can't you make her feel better?" he asked.

This made me think back to when Vihaan asked me if med school would've taught me anything about skincare.

"Eye doctor, kiddo, not a PCP," I smiled.

Leo didn't comment on that and simply continued eating while I went to check on my little princess. Riya's jealous that I don't call her "princess" anymore, so I've decided that the best solution is calling Elle "little princess".

Elle was asleep next to her mother. "How's she doing?" I asked.

"Her temperature went down. I still can't believe Mia flew out the best doctor from California to check up on her," Riya answered.

"It's nice to have a rich cousin." I kissed both of my princesses on the head before returning to my son.

Leo was washing his dishes when I returned.

"Good job! Thank you for doing that. We appreciate you helping out."

He smiled. "You're welcome, dad. Can I go play now?"

"Of course. Please, don't get your clothes dirty," I said, just as the doorbell rang.

"They're here!" Leo ran to the door and I had to remind him about safety again: "Kids don't answer the door. You have to let an adult open it."

Vihaan was there with Ezra. That was what I was expecting. What I *wasn't* expecting was Anaya with another child in her arms.

"That's a baby!" I exclaimed, dumbfounded.

"Seems you were smart enough for med school after all," Vihaan teased as I let them in.

I left to inform Riya, who was just as surprised as I was. She let Elle sleep while we went outside.

Ezra and Leo were playing with each other already when we got back.

"That's such a tiny baby!" Riya said, surprised. "Let me hold her, please!"

Anaya carefully placed the baby into Riya's arms. "Her name is Pari."

"That's beautiful. She's your angel!" I said, keeping an eye on the kids as well.

"She was tossed into a dumpster about three days after she was allowed to go home. We had told many people we were ready for a second kid to join our family, so one of them reached out to us about her and now we have our Pari," Vihaan said, looking at his baby.

I loved that they chose that name. Pari translated to angel, so it worked beautifully.

"How old is she now?" Riya asked.

"She's three weeks old," Anaya answered. "By the way, thanks for not asking why we didn't choose to adopt a son. We got that shit a lot from the Desi community. We wanted to improve a child's life, regardless of gender."

"Having a daughter is a blessing. Congratulations," I smiled. "You're twice as blessed."

Leo came to sit next to Vihaan. Even though Leo claims that Vihaan is his best friend, I've stopped trying to tell people at this rate.

"You want to hold her?" Vihaan asked.

He shook his head, saying he was scared. However, Riya still helped him hold her.

"So tiny," he admired. "I have three sisters to protect as the big brother."

I couldn't help but feel proud that he said that. He looked at me and said, "That's a lot of responsibility for a seven-year-old."

All four of us burst out laughing at his comment.

"You'll be the best brother," Riya told him.

Vihaan asked him if he was ready to go to the amusement park. Leo nodded as Ash walked in. Ash doesn't ring the doorbell, ever. He walks in like it's his place; since he's my brother, I have no problem with that. Riya never did, either.

"I have news!" He exclaimed from the doorway.

"I'm....that's a baby! Who's baby is that?" He asked.

"Ours. We adopted her," Vihaan answered.

"Damn! I thought I had news, but wow. She's so tiny. Can I hold her? Wait, let me wash my hands," he ran to the kitchen before returning and holding her.

We all waited for him to realize we wanted to know his news. It wasn't going to happen any time soon. He's busy with Pari.

I cleaned my throat after waiting for five minutes.

"Right! I proposed! Riya bhabi already knew last night. I wanted to tell you all today since I was going to see you."

The congratulations poured in for my younger brother. I still can't believe Riya knew before me. Again!

Leo was getting impatient, so those of us that signed up to go to the amusement park all piled into one car and drove off.

Both of our kids chose to stick with Ash. They probably get enough of us throughout the day.

We didn't take mainly big kid rides, as much as I would have loved.

"Varun." I turned to the familiar face.

"Nancy! How are you?" I asked, giving her a side hug.

"Good. How are you? Hi, Vihaan. How have you been."

"Good. Have two daughters that keep me busy," he answered.

Wait! She was expecting, wasn't she? Where's her kid?

"Congratulations," she said as Ryan joined her. "I had a miscarriage. I don't know if you heard."

"I'm so sorry," we both said.

"Thank you. What brings you both here?" Ryan asked.

"The kids. They wanted to do something.

What about you?" I asked.

"Abhi and Neeti were arguing over something, so I got the private jet and went on vacation."

Vihaan laughed before stepping away, saying his New Zealand friend was here. What's happening? Why is everyone here today?

"You have to come home with me. I never got to thank you properly for everything you did for Riya. I'm not taking no for an answer."

Riya

What does Varun mean by, I'm bringing company home? That's all he texted. Anaya had let her daughter nap and is now helping me out. I told her she didn't need to, but she insisted.

"You should go check on Elle. I'll finish up here," she said.

"I'm sure you want to be with Pari right now. You should go."

"She's napping. I got this. Trust me, I'm a chef's wife," she proudly smiled.

If Vihaan had heard her say, I could only imagine what would have happened. As long as it didn't happen in my house and there were no kids around.

"I still can't believe you put yourself at risk of marrying someone you didn't want to, only for Vihaan's safety."

Her smile disappeared. "I never wanted to hurt him. I love him so much, Riya. He's the perfect husband and the perfect dad. He's everything I could have asked for."

"I feel the same way about Varun. Come to think of it, the night of the roka, I constantly asked myself if I was making a mistake. This was a beautiful mistake and I'd make it repeatedly."

"So you did think it was a mistake?" She questioned.

"Yes. When he annoyed me with checking up on everything constantly," I laughed. "Now I have a beautiful life. I love it and that's something the past version of me never thought she'd be able to say."

"Surprise!" We turned to see who had walked into my house.

Oh my God!

"I did say I was bringing company," Varun smiled as I hugged Nancy and Ryan. "Hey, you forgot your husband!"

He hasn't changed at all. I thought four years later, with children four and seven, he would.

I shook my head as I walked past him.

Vihaan had left to see what Anaya was working on in the kitchen.

"Riya, don't ever let her in the kitchen. Ever! Keep yourself alive and everyone else," he smirked. "But anyways, we also have someone to meet up with, so we'll see you later. And I mean it. Nobody let her in the kitchen!"

They left with that. We'll be seeing them again next Saturday for the fourth of July.

Time flew by with Nancy and Ryan. Leo played with Elle, who seemed to be doing better after her nap.

I also invited them for the 4th, but they said Neeti already made plans that they agreed to. They said the three of them would be there next year.

"Three?" I asked. "Who are you leaving behind? Abhi or Neeti?"

"Both. I can't deal with their arguments. They love each other, but will annoy the other to no end. We meant that we would be here next year. I'm expecting again after four years," Nancy broke the news.

"Nancy! Congratulations! That's awesome," I told her.

"Thank you. I wanted to wait until I was physically and mentally prepared."

We carried on our conversations with joy. They stayed for dinner and left right after.

It was time to get Leo to bed. Elle would probably not fall asleep since she napped so much today. She was awake when Anaya was helping me in the kitchen but didn't come outside until her brother was there.

Varun got to work on getting him ready for bed. He still has to make sure he reads them a bedtime story. I don't think it will ever hit him that they're growing up.

Once Leo was asleep, I checked on Elle, gave her the medication, and let her watch some TV. When I knew she was ready for bed, I'd lay her down and he'd come to read to her.

"Riya," he said, getting my attention. There he goes using my name again. I thought we figured this out. Princess and little princess. What's so hard about that?

"Ya?"

"You should sleep. You've been up since early."

"I'll be fine. You can go to bed. I'll finish cleaning up."

He took the rag out of my hands. "Bedtime. Now.You'll get sick if you keep doing this. You need to let yourself rest. I got it."

I nodded, leaving to go change. I've been up since seven in the morning, checking up on Elle. My mood goes down when any of my kids gets sick.

As I lied down, I realized how exhausted I was. I would have been knocked out if Varun hadn't come inside.

When he lied down, I scooted closed for cuddles.

"Goodnight, princess. I love you."

There it is!

"I love you too. Goodnight."

He pulled me closer to him as if we weren't close enough. I laughed at his actions. I swear he's something else.

"Varun, You know you saved my life, right? I was going to take my life the day I met you. Now, I have a beautiful life I would have never thought possible growing up."

"I'll always remind you how beautiful you are, not that I don't do it daily. But I also have to say, my life wouldn't be close to beautiful without you in it. I love you so much. You're the perfect wife and the best mother I could have asked for our kids."

Yep, definitely didn't need to worry about whether I was making a mistake trusting him. Everyone's right, beautiful action- beautiful consequence.

Want to read what Riya read?

Check out *Contracted Together*
releasing February 11th, 2023.

Something about Zavian is off. I've not been living with him for too long, but I can pick up easily on people's changes. I had asked the driver, Ahren, and his bodyguard if anything had happened, but they had no idea.

I tossed and turned all night, trying to figure out what it could be. It most definitely had to be work-related. What else does this man even think about? If it's his mother doing something, I will have her buried away before he finds out where she went.

It's already four-eighteen in the morning. I might just call in sick since I haven't slept at all.

I heard something shatter loudly and ran to check on him. He doesn't seem like the type of person that would begin to throw things when stressed or angry. If he is, then I'm going to have to risk it. A little glass can't hurt me worse than I've been hurt already.

I didn't bother to knock and ran straight into his room. Where the hell is the light switch? I moved my hand around the wall, trying to find it. Bingo!

I turned the light, focusing only on him and not the interior of his room. He was still asleep, so maybe it was a night terror. Those are also caused by stress and lack of sleep. I know I'm not supposed to wake him up from that. I went to the bedside and picked up the glass pieces from the mug that had to have been accidentally knocked over.

I'll wait for him to wake up. I have to find a good doctor for this or even a therapist. He can't let work take his health.

"What're you doing?" he asked as I was picking up the glass.

"You're awake. How're you feeling?"

"Good, but why are you in my room?" He leaned onto his side to look at me. "Picking up...is that glass?"

I nodded, unfolding my hand to show the big pieces. "You knocked it over. I ran over to make sure you were alright."

He sat up, moving his hand across his face. "I woke you up, didn't I?"

"I couldn't sleep anyways," I told him, not wanting him to feel guilty. "You seemed to be having a bad dream. Was it about your dad again?"

He shook his head as I tossed the glass out in the trash. He patted the mattress for me to sit.

"I get a lot of different stuff. Sometimes it's about dad and sometimes about how my mother treated me. I was abused by her in multiple ways. She always called me a mistake since she didn't mean to have me. My brother and dad loved me, but she never did. It got worse after he passed and Ahren went to college. Ahren had barely finished his business degree when I ended up in the hospital. That night she almost took the abuse too far. Let's just say I was fortunate that the neighbors saw."

"Can I see?" I asked. "Your scars. Can I see them? I know I'm just a contract wife, but I'm human. I won't say anything if you say no."

"It's not that, Mona. I trust you more than I thought I would. Unfortunately, some of the scars are a bit lower, if you know what I mean?"

Okay, I'm definitely going to beat the shit out of his mother. That's her son! Is she stupid?

I took his hand in mine. "I understand. But if you get word that your mother has passed, I may have had something to do with it. Plus, you have money. You can bail me out."

"As much as I'd love to bail you out, I want to clarify that I'm still a virgin. I don't believe in sleeping around with people and nor was I ever assaulted in that sense. I don't know why she always wanted to beat me from the stomach down. I was on crutches for two months because she ran over my foot with the car. Told me to just stand there and reversed right over it. I didn't even get a chance to move with how fast she went. She told the doctor that someone else had done it. I wanted to tell the doctor everything, but that meant the backlash would be worse. I took all the beatings. I'm still taking them."

"She still hits you?" I asked in disbelief.

"Not physically. Now she's trying to hit where it'll hurt the most."

"Your business. She wants the title, right?"

He nodded. "But that's not what it is."

If not the business, then what? His brother?

"She's trying to get some paperwork done so I can't visit dad's grave. That's what hurts the most," he said as my heart shattered. "I'd give her the title in a heartbeat to keep dad. She took it too far, though, so now I'll keep everything."

"You do know you're not fighting alone, right? We're doing this together," I told him, still holding his hand.

"I know," he said. "And your hand is bleeding."

I looked down at my other hand and sure enough, it was bleeding out. How did I not feel the pain? I looked over at the time to see if I could bandage it. Four fifty-five. I sighed. "I have to get ready for work. I'll bandage it after I shower."

"You should call in. You didn't get any sleep, did you?"

I lied and said I did. Plus, what will I do at home alone if he doesn't take a day off? "I'll make you breakfast so you can warm it up before you go to work," I said, letting his hand go. "I have something to do afterward today, so I'll be late."

"You aren't going to get blood on your hands. Come straight home after work."

How did he figure that out?

I showed him my bleeding hand. "Too late, Mr. Malhotra. It seems getting blood on my hand is bound to happen."

For a second, I thought I saw the ghost of a smile on his face. I'll have to make it a mission to teach him how to smile again before the year ends.

About the Author

Beautiful Mistake is Jyoti's fourth novel after *The Chaos Within Us,Beautiful Consequence* and *The Chance We Took.* Her goal is to shed light onto topics considered taboo in the South Asian Communities through her writing. She is also the founder of SincerleyGeetMH.Carrd.co. Anticipate the release of *Contracted Together* in February 2023 and *Better Than Him* March 2023.

You can learn more about the author via:

- https://geetwrites.carrd.co/
- https://www.goodreads.com/author/show/22904762.Jyoti_Dhanota

Keep up to date by following her on instagram at https://www.instagram.com/geetisbooked/

Acknowledgments

The sequel is finally out! First book of 2023 I put out, I hope everyone enjoyed it. Be sure you are following me on Instagram because I do a giveaway for all the books I release with lots of freebies on the side.

Biggest thank you to Christine Cover Designs for the cover of this book as well. She had designed the cover of *Beautiful Mistake* and I'm so lucky to have found her.

My editors Jewel from Etsy, Viva Marie, and Gratimore Press. This book got looked at by two different sets of eyes for editing purposes, it would have been a mess without both of you.

Thank you for doing the layout of my book in both paperback and ebook.

To my readers, I hope you enjoyed this book and will check out the other novels that I have written.

www.ingramcontent.com/pod-product-compliance
Lightning Source LLC
LaVergne TN
LVHW010553160826
845677LV00013B/3116

* 9 7 9 8 3 7 4 3 7 1 6 1 1 *